DISNEP

Let It Go

A Twisted Tale

JEN CALONITA

AUTUMN
PUBLISHING

AUTUMN
PUBLISHING

Published in 2019
by Autumn Publishing
Cottage Farm
Sywell
NN6 0BJ
www.igloobooks.com

Autumn is an imprint of Bonnier Books UK

0819 001
2 4 6 8 10 9 7 5 3 1
ISBN 978-1-83852-703-7

Printed and manufactured in Italy

For my *Frozen*-loving partners in crime,
Joanie Cook and Kristen Marino

—J.C.

CHAPTER ONE

Elsa

"Presenting Princess Elsa of Arendelle!"

Elsa stepped out of the shadow of her parents and into the sun. Her people were waiting, welcoming her presence in the village square with thunderous applause. There must have been hundreds of subjects gathered, young and old, waving flags with the royal family crest, throwing flowers, and cheering. Children sat high on their fathers' shoulders, some people stood atop carriages, and others leaned out nearby windows. Everyone wanted to get a better look at the princess. Her parents were used to interacting with their kingdom, but at eighteen, she had only recently been invited to join them on official outings.

Truth be told, she still preferred to live life in the shadows, but duty called.

"Welcome, Princess Elsa!" the people shouted. Elsa and her parents were standing on a raised platform that had been constructed for the event. It overlooked the large courtyard outside the castle gates, giving her a good vantage point, but it also made her feel as if she was on display. That was probably the point.

"Look! It's Arendelle's princess," she heard a mother tell her small daughter. "Isn't she beautiful? Offer her your gift."

The little girl was standing in front of the stage holding a bouquet of purple heather, which was Elsa's favorite flower. Every time she reached up to hand the bouquet to Elsa, she was knocked back by the crowd.

Elsa looked to her mother for guidance. The queen gave a small nod, and Elsa descended the steps, holding the bottom of her pale blue dress, which she had paired with a matching fitted jacket for the occasion. She and her mother shared similar light eyes, but she looked more like her papa with her light hair, which she usually wore in a braided bun at the nape of her neck.

"Thank you for the lovely flowers," Elsa told the child, graciously accepting the bouquet before stepping back up onto the platform to speak to the crowd. Her father had been teaching her the unique power of presenting to a large group.

"We are pleased you could all join us this afternoon as Axel Ludenburg unveils the sculpture of the royal family he has so graciously gifted our kingdom," she began. The people applauded. "One note before the unveiling: as Mr. Ludenburg has spent years working on this piece, I suspect I will look much younger molded in bronze than I do standing before you today."

The crowd chuckled and Elsa glanced back at her father proudly. That line had been her idea. He gave her an encouraging smile.

"His contribution to this kingdom is paramount." Elsa smiled at the sculptor. "And now, without further ado, I would like to introduce Mr. Ludenburg." Elsa moved aside to allow the older gentleman to join them.

"Thank you, Princess." Mr. Ludenburg bowed to her, his white beard almost touching his knees; then he turned to the crowd. "I am thankful to King Agnarr, Queen Iduna, and our fair princess, Elsa, for allowing me to create a sculpture in their honor. It is my hope that this piece will greet every guest who journeys from villages near and far to visit Arendelle's castle and stand inside its gates." He looked to his assistant, who dashed forward, untied the rope around the sheet concealing the sculpture where it stood in the middle of a fountain, and pulled it off. "May I present the royal family of Arendelle!"

There was a loud gasp from the crowd, followed by rapt applause.

It was the first time the king, the queen, and Elsa had seen the completed sculpture. Elsa remembered sitting for Mr. Ludenburg's sketches when she was around eleven, but she'd almost forgotten he'd been working on it until recently, when her father told her she'd be the one to speak at the royal engagement for its unveiling.

"It's beautiful," Elsa told Mr. Ludenburg. And she meant it.

Seeing the bronze sculpture was like looking at a moment frozen in time. Mr. Ludenburg had molded the royal family perfectly. The youthful king looked regal in his crown and robe as he stood next to the beautiful queen in her tiara and fine dress. Nestled between them was their only child, Princess Elsa of Arendelle, who looked much younger than her eighteen years.

Seeing the image of her eleven-year-old self flooded Elsa with emotion. Life in the castle had been lonely for her as an only child. Her parents were busy with kingdom affairs, and while she had numerous studies, she still spent a lot of time roaming the empty rooms, watching the hours tick by. Of course, her parents had found her playmates in their stewards' and noblemen's children, but it wasn't the same as having a sibling to grow up with and confide in. This was a weight she kept to herself, never wanting to burden her parents with her feelings. Her mother had been unable to have more children after Elsa.

"Isn't the sculpture of us lovely, Mama?" Elsa asked.

Her mother was standing quietly beside her. Elsa watched her blue eyes take in every inch of the bronze statue before she gave a deep, almost inaudible, sigh. When she glanced at Elsa, her eyes seemed sad. "It truly is," she said, squeezing her daughter's hand. "It's a lovely portrait of our family and who we are. Isn't it?" she added to the king.

For such a joyous occasion, her parents seemed slightly melancholy. Was it that the statue reflected a time when they were much younger? Were they sad to think how quickly time had passed? Her father was always talking about the day when she would take the throne, even though he was still a vibrant king. Elsa wondered what made them sad, but she kept her thoughts to herself. It wasn't her place to question her parents in public.

"Yes, it is quite the honor," Papa replied, and looked at Elsa. He seemed to want to say something more but held his tongue. "You should thank our subjects for coming, Elsa," he said finally. "We're hosting a dinner in Mr. Ludenburg's honor back at the castle, so we must return and get ready to greet all our guests."

"Yes, Papa," Elsa said, and did as she was told.

———

"To Axel Ludenburg and his fine work!" the king said, holding his goblet high above the banquet table in the Great Hall. The other guests did the same.

"To Axel!" they shouted, and clinked glasses.

The food was plentiful, the company boisterous, and the seating at the long table at capacity. The king had asked Lord Peterssen, his most trusted friend, to join them at the celebration. Mr. Ludenburg's family was there, too, having traveled by ship from the nation of Weselton, a longtime trade partner of Arendelle. The Duke of Weselton had come with them, and seated himself next to Elsa.

"And to Arendelle and Weselton!" the Duke added. He had a big mouth for such a small man. Elsa couldn't help noticing he was at least a foot shorter than most guests at the table when he stood up. "Long may our countries grow together and prosper!"

"To Arendelle and Weselton!" everyone echoed.

Elsa clinked glasses with her mother.

"I'm so glad we finally have a chance to dine together," the Duke said to Mama as the supper plates were taken away and the staff prepared to bring out dessert. "It is a pleasure to meet the princess and witness Arendelle's bright future." His brow furrowed. "I've long noticed she doesn't come to many public events."

Elsa politely returned his smile but said nothing. One

of the roles of being a princess, as Mama kept reminding her, was to listen to people but wait to speak till something important needed to be said.

"Elsa is so busy with her studies that we haven't asked her to join us on many public outings yet," Mama told him, and looked at Mr. Ludenburg. "But of course, we couldn't have her miss the unveiling of our family sculpture. That is what this whole evening is all about: family."

Elsa covered her mouth to hide her smirk. Her mother had a knack for keeping conversations focused.

This was Elsa's first time meeting the Duke of Weselton. Already she could tell she preferred the Duke of Blakeston, who had kind eyes and always came to the castle with pocketfuls of chocolate, which he snuck to the princess during particularly boring dinner discussions.

Correction: *important negotiations*. As her mother kept reminding her, she needed to be ready for the throne when her time came. These days she divided her time between lessons on handwriting, science, and statecraft with her governess, and Papa's meetings. She was also now old enough to attend the banquets held at the castle, of which there were many. Gone were the days when she was trotted out to say hello to guests, then sent to another room to have supper. Life was less lonely, but she still longed for someone her own age to confide in. The days of hosting playmates were long over.

"Agreed, agreed! But she is too much of an asset to be locked away." The Duke pounded the table as if to make a point. He moved so much when he talked his toupee kept flipping up on the back of his head.

"Fine point, Your Grace," said Lord Peterssen, joining the conversation. "She's a young lady now and ready to take part in the kingdom's conversations."

Elsa smiled at him. Papa and Lord Peterssen were so close he wasn't just an advisor; he was family. Elsa had always thought of him like an uncle. And like an uncle, he had warned Elsa before the dinner about the Duke's tendency to pry.

"Exactly!" the Duke agreed. "Princess Elsa, I'm sure your studies taught you a lot about fjords and how instrumental they can be." Elsa nodded. "Well, in Weselton, it was my grandfather who discovered the first fjord. It is because of him that we . . ."

The Duke droned on and on till Lord Peterssen cleared his throat. "Fascinating, Your Grace! Perhaps we can finish this conversation later? I believe dessert is being served." He turned away before the Duke could interrupt him. "Mr. Ludenburg, I hope you are still hungry!"

As if on cue, the staff appeared at the doors with platters of fruit and sweets, which they placed on the table.

"We have all these treats and more in Weselton," the

Duke piped up as he helped himself to a piece of cake and two cookies.

Elsa knew it was wrong of her to think it, but "Weselton" sounded a lot like "Weaseltown," and the Duke did have a weasel-like way about him. She glanced at Papa. Had he ever noticed this connection between the Duke and his country's name? His thoughts were always veiled. At the moment, he was having a side conversation with Mr. Ludenburg's wife. Lord Peterssen was speaking with the sculptor himself about his next project, which left the Duke, Mama, and Elsa unengaged.

"Your Majesty, you have a lovely daughter," the Duke said, making Elsa immediately feel guilty about her thoughts. "She will make a fine queen."

"Thank you," Mama said. "She truly will."

"My parents have taught me well," Elsa added, smiling at Mama. "When my day comes, I know I am ready to lead Arendelle."

The Duke looked at her with interest. "Yes! Yes! I'm sure. It's just a shame you're the only heir. Why, in the Southern Isles, the king has thirteen sons in line for the throne."

Elsa clutched her goblet on the table to keep from saying something she would regret. Strangely, the goblet was ice cold. "Sir, I hardly think that's—"

Mama cut her off. "What Elsa is trying to say is, that is a lot of heirs." Mama was seemingly unperturbed, having been asked about this before. "My fate was to have only one child, but the world is full of surprises." She looked at Elsa, her eyes shiny. "I know that she will be fine in the future."

"Our kingdom only needs one strong leader," Elsa added, her voice firm. "They already have that in me."

The Duke frowned. "Yes, but if anything were to prevent you from taking the throne—"

"We are fully prepared to lead Arendelle into the future, Duke, I assure you," Mama said with a smile.

The Duke scratched his head, his toupee shifting slightly. He looked from the queen to Elsa over his spectacles. "She will be of age in a few years. Are there any potential suitors on the horizon? A match between our two nations or with another trade partner could be prosperous indeed."

Elsa stared at the napkin in her lap. She felt her cheeks burning.

"Elsa has plenty of time to find a suitor," Mama said. "For now, we just want our daughter to focus her attention on her duties to this kingdom."

That statecraft test her governess was giving her in the morning was a lot more pressing than finding a suitor. "Thank you for thinking of me, Your Grace," Elsa added. "When I do find a suitor, I'm sure you'll be one of the first to know." She was being wry, but the Duke seemed pleased with her response. Mama gave her a reproachful look, but Elsa couldn't help herself.

When the Duke finally retired and Mr. Ludenburg and his family had said their goodbyes, the king, the queen, and Elsa headed to their private chambers.

"You handled yourself well," Mama told her. "You were excellent at conversation and you impressed the Duke with your knowledge of trade negotiations."

"He looked surprised I knew as much as I did," Elsa said. Her shoulders felt tense, as if she'd been carrying the weight of her kingdom on them all evening. She was starting to get a headache and she longed for the quiet of her room.

"I'm very proud of you," Papa said, letting his guard down for the first time all evening. He smiled at Mama and placed his hand on her arm.

She loved watching her parents together. They still looked so in love. It was hard not to envy the connection they had with each other.

"You will make an excellent queen someday, Elsa," he added.

"Thank you, Papa," she replied, but didn't think anything of it.

Becoming queen was a lifetime away.

CHAPTER TWO

Elsa

"On Mondays, subjects are invited to meet with your mother and me to discuss any concerns they have for the kingdom. I think it's best if we keep a standing appointment. You and Lord Peterssen can meet with them and listen to their concerns. Be compassionate and considerate and promise to pass any grievances on to us when we return. Now, on Tuesdays . . . Elsa? Are you listening?"

"Yes, Papa," Elsa said, but in truth her mind was elsewhere.

They were sitting in the library, discussing his weekly schedule, but she was distracted. She'd spent a lot of time in that room over the years, and even as a little girl, she had felt her mind wander when she was around all those books. The dark room was lined with shelves filled with books from floor to ceiling. Her father was always reading and had several books open on the desk. That day he was looking at one that didn't seem to be written in their language. It was filled with symbols and drawings of trolls. She longed to know what her father was studying, but didn't ask.

What he wanted her to know right then was what to do in his and Mama's absence. They were scheduled to go on a diplomatic voyage for at least two weeks in a few days' time. Elsa couldn't remember when they'd ever been away that long before. There was a part of her that was nervous. She knew she would keep busy between her own work and her father's appointments, but she missed her parents already and they hadn't even left yet.

Her father folded his hands in his lap and gave her a small smile. "What's the matter, Elsa?"

Even when it was just the two of them, her father still seemed like a king. It wasn't just that he always dressed the part, in his uniform with a multitude of medals, and with the Arendelle crest hanging from his neck. Whether he was speaking to a foreign dignitary or thanking one of the castle workers, his manner always seemed royal. He was powerful and in control even when he didn't have to be—like during a game of chess with his only daughter. She still felt shy sometimes. Was that just who she was, or was it that she didn't have many people her age to converse with? Speaking to the large crowd at Mr. Ludenburg's event had made her nervous. Her father never looked uneasy. Did that kind of confidence come with time?

"Nothing," Elsa lied. It wasn't possible to put all she was thinking into a few words.

"Ah, but it is something." He leaned back in his chair and studied her closely. "I know that look. You are thinking about something. Your mother says I get a far-off look in my eye when I'm doing the same thing. You, my child, are a lot like me."

"Really?" Elsa brushed an invisible strand of hair out of her eyes.

She was proud to take after Papa. She adored her mother and loved spending time with her, but often she couldn't tell what her mother was thinking. Sometimes Mama would lose her train of thought when she came into Elsa's room, or start saying something and abruptly stop. There was a lingering sadness about her that Elsa could never put her finger on.

Take that day, for example. For years, Mama had always disappeared for one full day every other month. Elsa had no clue where she went, and neither Papa nor Mama ever explained. This time, Elsa couldn't help herself. She was tired of the secrets, so she finally got the courage to ask Mama if she could join her on her outing. Mama looked surprised, then worried, then apologetic. "I wish I could take you, darling, but this is something I must do alone." She had touched Elsa's cheek, her eyes welling with tears, which only confused Elsa more. "I wish you could come." Yet she had gone alone.

With Papa, things were different. "I'm not thinking of anything important, Papa. Really."

"Something is on your mind, Elsa," he insisted. "What is it?"

She felt foolish saying she didn't want them to go away, but that was part of it. With them gone, Arendelle was in her hands. Yes, the advisors and Lord Peterssen were there if anything important needed to be taken care of, but she was the face of the kingdom in their absence, and she could feel the weight of that pressing on her. Before long, they'd return and life would be as it had been before, but this trip seemed like a steadfast reminder that someday she would have to rule on her own. The thought was terrifying.

"Elsa?"

Two weeks alone in this large castle. Elsa wasn't sure she could bear it. "Do you really have to go?" she asked. She couldn't help it.

"You'll be fine, Elsa," he promised.

There was a knock on the door. "Your Majesty?" Kai entered. He'd been working in the castle since before Elsa was born. While the king ran the kingdom, Kai ran the castle. He knew where everything and everyone were always supposed to be. He was such an important part of the king's and queen's lives that he even had a room adjacent to their chambers. Kai pulled at a loose thread on the jacket of the green suit he always wore. "The Duke of Weselton is here to see you."

"Thank you. Please tell him I'll meet him in the council chambers shortly," Papa said.

"Yes, Your Majesty." Kai smiled at Elsa and disappeared.

Papa turned to her. "You look like you have more to say."

Too much to share in just a few short moments. "I was trying to decide what to serve at the session with the subjects," Elsa said instead. "Do you serve food? I think it would be nice to nourish them after their journey to the castle to see us. Don't you think?"

He smiled. "I think that's a splendid idea. I've always been fond of your krumkake cookies."

"*My* cookies?" Elsa couldn't recall ever baking for her father. "You're giving me credit for something Olina must have made, but I'm happy to request them."

Olina was in charge of the kitchen in the castle and oversaw all the workers. When Elsa was a girl, she had often snuck away to the kitchen to sit with her. She hadn't done that in a long time. And she didn't remember ever baking cookies.

Papa's brow furrowed. "Right. Still, they'd be delicious. Maybe Olina will make them for our guests."

Elsa started to rise. "Is there anything else, Papa?"

"Yes." He stood up. "Before you go, there is something I wanted to give you. Follow me, if you don't mind."

Elsa followed Papa to her parents' bedroom and watched as he walked to a bookcase along one wall and pressed on one of the books. The entire wall opened like a door. A small darkened chamber was behind it. Elsa strained to see where he was going, but Papa didn't ask her to follow. The castle was full of hidden hallways and rooms like that one. Papa and she had played hide-and-seek in a few once upon a time, but she knew now they were meant to shuttle the royal family to safety if there was an invasion.

Moments later, her father came out with a large green wooden box. It was the size of a breakfast tray and was hand-painted with white and gold rosemaling of the golden crocus, Arendelle's official flower. The top of the box had a beautiful arch to it.

"I want you to have this." He placed the box on the table in front of her. Her fingers traced the gold family crest etched into the rounded top. The box was identical to the lockbox her father kept on his desk and carried with him to meet with his advisors. It usually held important decrees to be signed as well as private papers and letters from the militia and nearby kingdoms. It had been instilled in her since she was small that the box should never be tampered with.

"May I?" she asked, her hand hovering over the latch. Her father nodded.

The lockbox was empty. The interior was lined with rich green velvet.

"This box was made for your monarchy," he said, and she looked up in surprise. "As you are next in line to the throne and just a few years away from coming of age, your mother and I felt it was time you had your own for safekeeping."

"Papa, it's beautiful," she said. "But I don't need one now."

"No," he said softly. "But someday you will, and we wanted you to be prepared. Kai and the staff know the lockbox by sight and know its contents are private. Whatever you put inside this box is for your eyes only, Elsa. Your secrets are safe in here. For now, I suggest you keep this in your chambers." His eyes searched hers for understanding.

Elsa ran her fingers along the green velvet interior. "Thank you, Papa."

He placed his hand atop hers. "It may not feel like it

now, but someday your whole life will change in ways you can't possibly imagine." He hesitated. "Promise me when it does, if I'm not here to guide you—"

"Papa—"

He cut her off. "Promise me that when that day comes, you will look to this box for guidance."

Look to it for guidance? It was a box. A beautiful box, but a box nonetheless. Still, it was a big step to be given a lockbox like the ones Papa and the kings and queens before him had used. "I promise," she said.

He kissed her on the forehead. "Put it somewhere safe."

Elsa picked up the box and walked to her parents' bedroom door. Papa followed her into the hallway, watching her. "I will," she promised.

Papa smiled, and went back to his work in the library.

Elsa walked back to her room with the lockbox nestled in her arms. The air was warm, and though little breeze came through the open windows, the sounds of the village drifted inside. Elsa lingered at a nearby window, staring over the castle walls and the courtyard to the world beyond. The village was alive and full of people. Horses and carriages came and went. The fountain that held their statue near the castle gates shot water high into the air like a geyser. Children were splashing in the fountain fully dressed, trying to stay cool. She watched as a mother pulled her son out of the fountain and scolded him. Despite the tongue-lashing, the boy looked like he was having fun. When was the last time Elsa had done that?

She wished Mama were there to have tea with that afternoon. It was a pity to sit alone in the castle on such a warm summer afternoon. Where was Mama on a day this spectacular? Why hadn't she let Elsa join her?

"Do you need something, Princess Elsa?" Gerda asked. "Water, perhaps? It's so hot today!"

Like Kai, Gerda had been around since before Elsa was born. She made sure Elsa was always well taken care of. At the moment, she was carrying a tray of goblets with cold water. Elsa suspected they were for her father and the Duke.

"Thank you, Gerda, I'm fine," Elsa said.

Gerda hurried past. "Okay. As long as you're staying cool. I don't want you overheating!"

Elsa kept walking, holding the box tighter. She needed to find something to do to pass the time till Mama returned. Maybe Gerda was right: she needed to stay cool. She could take a walk around the courtyard. Or perhaps she'd read for a spell. Her father had given her some books to look over that explained arrangements Arendelle had with other kingdoms.

She knew he wanted her to become familiar with things for the future, but at the moment, reading up on the kingdom's dealings didn't sound like fun at all. Elsa opened the doors to her room and made her way to her childhood desk. She placed the lockbox on top of it, staring at it for a moment. Alongside her things, the green box looked out of place.

Maybe a box that sacred wasn't meant to be out in the open. What important papers did she have to place in it? What correspondence did she engage in? No, for now she wasn't queen. The box wasn't needed, and hopefully it wouldn't be for a very long time. She took it to her hope chest, her right hand grazing the letter *E* hand-painted on the lid, and placed it safely inside, covering it with a quilt her mother had made her when she was a baby. Then she closed the lid. A moment later, Elsa grabbed a book from her nightstand, the lockbox all but forgotten.

CHAPTER THREE

Elsa

Elsa heard knocking and woke with a start. The late-afternoon sun was casting shadows that tiptoed along the walls. She must have fallen asleep reading.

Gerda poked her head into the room. "Oh, Princess Elsa!" she said in surprise. "I didn't mean to wake you. I was just coming to get you for supper before I called on your parents."

"It's all right. I'm up," Elsa said, stretching her arms wide. If her parents were joining her for dinner, that meant her father's meeting with the Duke of Weselton was done and her mother had returned. "Why don't I call on them for you?"

Gerda walked to Elsa's bed and started to smooth out the quilt and fix the pillows. "Thank you, Princess!"

Elsa's room was above her parents' chambers, which were above the Great Hall, where dinner would be served. While Gerda tidied up, Elsa headed down the stairs and stopped short when she heard them arguing. Her parents never fought, and she was so surprised, she wound up eavesdropping.

"There must be something we can do! We can't continue like this!"

It was her mother talking.

"Iduna, we've been over this time and time again." Her father sounded frustrated. "We don't have a choice. We must wait."

"I'm tired of waiting! We've lived like this for far too long!"

"When it comes to magic, there is no timeline. He warned us about this."

Magic? Magic was part of a child's imagination. The stuff of storybooks. Why would her parents be talking about something that didn't exist?

"We were desperate. We didn't think. We should have tried to change their fates. Maybe if we appealed to Grand Pabbie again . . ."

"No! We can't be seen there. Even your travels to the village are getting too risky. What if someone learned where you were going? Who you were seeing? Do you know what would happen if she were brought here?"

Who are they talking about? Elsa strained to hear more. Was this about where Mama disappeared to on her outings? Nothing they were saying made sense.

"I am always discreet, and I won't stop visiting." Her mother sounded defiant. "We've missed so much already."

"It was the only way. You and I both know that. The magic will break soon."

"It's been over ten years and it hasn't waned! It isn't fair to any of us, especially Elsa."

She perked up. What did this have to do with her?

"Elsa is fine."

"She's *not* fine, Agnarr. She's lonely."

Yes! Elsa wanted to cry out. *I am lonely.* Her mother knew her innermost thoughts. It almost made her want to cry with relief. But she didn't understand what that had to do with their argument.

"We will introduce her to more people. The Duke of Weselton mentioned a prince he thought she might connect with. We've let her start coming to royal outings. The important thing is she's safe. They both are. Isn't that what we wanted?"

"She deserves to know what she's capable of, Agnarr."

"She will when the time is right. We haven't seen any sign she still can—"

"There you are, Princess!" Gerda came up behind her

and Elsa jumped. "I was wondering if you had gotten lost. Olina is ready to serve supper. Have you spoken to your parents?"

"I . . ." Elsa's cheeks flushed as her parents stepped into the hallway, looking from Elsa to Gerda.

Her mother kissed her forehead. "How long have you been standing there?" she asked.

"I had just reached your door when Gerda arrived," she lied.

Her mother's face relaxed. "I missed you today." She linked arms with Elsa and started walking with her down the hall to the staircase. "I want to hear what you did while I was gone."

"Nothing much." It was the truth, yet Elsa knew there was also much she wasn't saying. Her parents talked about banal things on their walk to supper, but Elsa couldn't concentrate. She kept thinking about their argument, and what her father had said. *Do you know what would happen if she were brought here?*

Elsa couldn't help wondering: who was "she"?

CHAPTER FOUR

Anna

Her bed was warm and cozy, and that incessant knocking seemed far away. Anna wiped the drool from her mouth and tried to keep dreaming, but it was hard. Someone kept interrupting.

"Anna?"

Her name sounded like a whisper on the wind. It was followed by more annoying knocking. "Anna?"

"Huh?" Anna pulled a piece of wet hair from her mouth and sat up.

"Sorry to wake you, but . . ."

"No, no, no, you didn't." Anna yawned, her eyes still closed. "I've been up for hours."

Normally she would have been. She always rose before the sun to help her parents prepare bread. Their shop,

Tomally's Baked Goods, churned out dozens of loaves and bakery items a day. But the previous night she'd had trouble sleeping and her dreams were restless. She kept calling for someone, but she couldn't remember who it was, just that she missed this person. Anna felt herself starting to drift off again.

"Anna?"

She let out a loud snore and jolted awake again. "What?"

"Time to get ready. Freya is coming this morning."

"Of course," Anna said, her eyes starting to close again. "Freya."

Wait. What?

Her eyes opened wide. "Freya's coming!"

Anna practically leapt out of bed and skidded across the floor in her bare feet. She didn't bother looking in the mirror. Her long red hair, which she had unbraided the night before, couldn't be that messy, could it? Hmmm . . . maybe she'd give it a quick glance before she pulled off her nightdress. She looked in the mirror. Not good. Her hair looked like a bird's nest.

Did she have time to fix it?

She had to fix it.

Where was her brush?

It should have been on the desk like it always was, but it wasn't there. Where was it?

Think, Anna. She remembered brushing her hair the morning before at the window seat, because it had the best view of Arendelle. Looking at Arendelle made her start dreaming about Arendelle and what she'd do when she someday moved there. She'd have her own bake shop, of course, and her cookies would be so popular that people would be lined up day and night to purchase them. She'd meet new people and make friends, and it all sounded so glorious she had started singing and spinning around the room with the hairbrush . . . Oh! Now she remembered where she had flung it. She knelt down and looked under her bed. Anna retrieved the brush and ran it through her hair as she walked around her room.

The hand-painted armoire matched the rosemaling on her desk, her bed, and her pink quilt. She and her mother had painted the pieces together. Her father had made her the rocking chair she sat in when she read, usually while she snuggled under her soft white blanket. But her favorite gift he'd made was the wooden Arendelle Castle he'd carved for her twelfth birthday. She kept it on the window seat, where she admired it day and night. Her pink room wasn't large, but she loved it. Hanging on the front of the armoire was the new royal-blue apron with red and green embroidery that her mother had made her. She'd been saving it for Freya's next visit, and that visit was today!

Her parents were so busy with the bakery they didn't socialize much, but her mother always made time for visits from her best friend, Freya. They'd been friends since they were girls, and they loved spending time together. Freya usually visited them in Harmon every other month, and Anna, her mother, and Freya would spend the whole day together, baking and talking. Anna loved hearing Freya talk about Arendelle, where she worked as a seamstress, and she loved when Freya brought her presents! There was that porcelain doll, the dark chocolate that melted on her tongue like ice, and the green silk party dress from overseas that had hung in her closet for two years. She didn't have anywhere to wear a dress that nice, since she spent her days covered in flour and butter stains. A dress like that deserved to go to a party with dancing, nice lighting, lots of talking, and *no* flour spills. They had parties in the village, but Anna was one of the only fifteen-year-olds in town. She assumed Arendelle had a lot more young people than Harmon did.

She pulled on her white dress shirt and green jumper, grabbed the apron, and finished brushing her hair, tugging at a particularly tough knot.

There was another knock on the door. "Anna!"

"Coming!" The sun was already starting to rise outside her window, and she had chores to do before Freya arrived. Freya was never late, while Anna tended to get distracted and show up a few minutes behind schedule no matter how punctual she tried to be.

Anna grabbed her shoes off the floor and hopped to the door, trying to move and get them on at the same time. She almost knocked over her father, Johan, who was patiently waiting outside her door.

"Papa!" Anna hugged him. "I'm sorry!"

"It's quite all right," he said, patting her back.

He was a round man, shorter than his daughter by at least a foot, and he always smelled like the mint leaves he chewed on constantly. (He had an upset stomach most days.) He'd been bald as long as Anna could remember, but the look suited him.

"Why didn't you remind me Freya was coming?" Anna asked as she tried in vain to smooth out her hair.

Her father's chuckle was deep, rising from his round belly. (He always said he taste-tested as many cookies as he sold.) "Anna, we told you twice last night and every day last week."

"Right!" Anna agreed, although she wasn't sure she remembered. The day before, she had delivered two cakes to Wandering Oaken's Trading Post and Sauna for his twins' birthday (Anna insisted they each get their own cake), taken krumkake to the village hall for the assembly meeting, and whipped up a new batch of her famous snowman cookies to keep up with demand. They were a kid favorite, even in the summer.

Freya loved them, too. She always asked for a dozen to take back with her when she left. Anna wondered if there were any snowman cookies left to give her.

"I should help Ma get ready," she told her father, and hurried down the stairs. She ran through their cozy family room and the small kitchen, then burst through the door that led to the bakery, which was attached to their home. A short woman with brown hair was already at the wooden table, mixing flour and eggs in a bowl. She looked up at Anna and smiled.

"It's about time you got down here." Her mother kissed her cheek and pushed a strand of wispy hair behind Anna's right ear, then straightened Anna's apron. She always wanted Anna to look nice when Freya visited.

"I know, I'm sorry," Anna said, spinning around and checking the baked goods set out for purchase on the counter. As she'd suspected, the snowman tray was empty. "And I'm out of my cookies! Freya loves them."

"I'm already mixing up the batter for a batch." Her mother's brown eyes looked tired.

It was getting harder and harder for her to work such long hours in the bakery. Anna tried to compensate for the work between her studies the best she could, but her parents were insistent that she focus on her schoolwork even when school wasn't in session. Papa kept telling her, "Riches come and go, but no one can take away your education." She understood, but that meant her days were as long as theirs were sometimes: rise early; bake; do chores; go to school or do home study and work on reading, writing, and mathematics; work at the bakery; then collapse and do it all over again the next day. It didn't leave much time for things like friends. That was why she looked forward to Freya's visits: they felt like a glimpse of the world beyond Harmon.

"We can make some with Freya today," her mother said.

"Good idea!" Anna took a swipe of batter with her finger and licked it. Her mother rapped her lightly with a spoon. "Sorry! But you always say a cook should taste what they make."

Her mother chuckled. "True. You certainly keep me on my toes, Anna Bear."

Anna kissed her mom on the cheek. "That's a good thing, right? Can you imagine life without me, Ma?"

Her mother stopped mixing and looked at her, the smile slipping off her face. She touched Anna's chin. "No, I cannot. But that day is coming, I'm sure."

Anna didn't say anything. She felt bad when her mother talked like that. That was why she didn't tell her about her plan to leave Harmon and move to Arendelle when she turned eighteen. She loved Harmon and its people, but it was small compared to other villages, and the world was a big place. She longed to see what life was like where the royal family lived.

"Can you see if we have enough tea?" her mother asked.

Anna checked the pantry, where they kept their dry goods. "I don't see any tea."

"Why don't you run to the market, then?" Her mother measured a scoop of sugar out of a container and added it to the bowl. "I always like to have tea on when she arrives. Freya has such a long journey. Can you think of anything else we need?"

Freya liked to set out early for her visits. She left Arendelle before dawn, so she usually hadn't yet had breakfast when she arrived. "Ma, do you think she'd like eggs?"

Her mother smiled. "That's a lovely idea."

Anna slipped off her shoes and put on her boots before her mother even finished the sentence. She grabbed her violet cape by the door. "I'll be fast."

"Anna, you are never fast," her mother said with a chuckle.

"You'll see—I'll be quick this time." Anna slipped out the door, took the bucket near the stoop, and headed down the street. First she'd stop at the market for tea; then she'd head to the farm a little ways away for the eggs. The sky was a sea of blues, much like the ocean in the distance, and the air felt warm, but not sticky. One good thing about life in the mountains, so Anna was repeatedly told, was that it was never as hot as it was in Arendelle. Mountain air was much cooler and life was much quieter. Anna snuck another glance at the mountainside, her eyes searching for Arendelle far below. She wondered what people were doing down there at that exact moment. Anna heard someone talking and stopped short, her bucket still swinging.

"What do you want, Sven?"

Ma called her a social butterfly. Papa called her Harmon's official greeter. She truly did like talking to people, and this was a voice she didn't recognize from their small village. It was only a few rows of houses, clustered tightly together on the mountainside overlooking Arendelle. Each one was a different bright color—green, blue, red. The bakery was orange. Anna knew the inhabitants of every one of those houses. The person speaking wasn't one of them.

"Give me a snack!" This was a second voice, much deeper than the first.

Curious, Anna rounded the corner to the market and saw a boy about her own age standing there. He was with a large reindeer hooked up to a wagon holding big blocks of ice. When school was in session, she met boys and girls of various ages, but she'd never seen this boy before. Oaken lived high in the mountains and his kids didn't come to Harmon often, but this didn't look like one of his children, either. The boy in front of her had shaggy blond hair and was wearing a deep-blue shirt with the sleeves rolled up, dark pants, and beige boots. Most important, he seemed to be *talking* to a reindeer.

"What's the magic word?" he asked the reindeer.

Men moved around them, busy carrying crates of vegetables that would be sold at the market. Anna watched the boy swipe a bunch of carrots from a crate when no one was looking. He held one high in the air above the reindeer.

"Please!" he said, putting on a deeper voice.

Anna watched as the reindeer bit at the carrot swinging above his snout.

"Ah, ah, ah!" The boy pulled the carrot away. "Share!" Next, the boy took a bite of the carrot, broke the rest in two pieces, and gave the other half to the reindeer.

Okay, that was gross, but intriguing. The boy was talking to and for the reindeer. Strange. She couldn't help giggling. The boy looked up with a start and caught her staring.

Anna inhaled sharply. Should she say hi? Run? This was her chance to meet someone her own age—even if he had just pinched some carrots. She should say hi. She stepped forward.

The sound of hooves pounding against the cobblestones

made her jump back. A wagon squeaked to a stop in front of her, and men quickly began unloading vegetables and taking them into the market.

I need to get tea and eggs! Look at me getting distracted. She had promised her mother she would hurry, and there she was, dawdling again. Still, maybe she could say hello on her way into the market. She walked around the horses to see the boy. He was gone.

Not meant to meet, I guess. Anna sighed, but she didn't have time to linger. She ran inside to purchase the tea, put it in her bag, and then ran down the road with her bucket. Mrs. Aagard, the cobbler's wife, was sweeping her stairs.

"Good morning, Mrs. Aagard!" Anna called.

"Morning, Anna! Thanks again for the bread yesterday," the woman said.

"My pleasure." Anna rushed onward, past another row of homes, and found her way to the farm where they kept their chicken coop. She opened the netting to collect a fresh batch of eggs. "Morning, Erik, Elin, and Elise," she greeted the hens. "I've got to move quick today. Freya is coming!" She gathered at least a dozen eggs, closed up the coop, and carefully carried the bucket and the tea back to the house.

An older man was pulling a cart with flowers down the street. "Morning, Anna!"

"Morning, Erling!" Anna called. "Gorgeous blooms today. Do you have my favorite?"

Erling produced two stems of golden crocuses. The yellow flowers were as bright as the sun. Anna inhaled their sweet aroma. "Thank you! Come by later for some fresh bread. First batch should be out of the oven midmorning."

"Thank you, Anna! I will!" he said, and Anna hurried along, trying not to crack the eggs or stop again. She had a habit of stopping to talk. A lot.

"Ma! I got the eggs and the tea! Is Freya here yet?" Anna called, walking through the door. Before she could close it, a carriage pulled up in front of the house. Freya had arrived.

CHAPTER FIVE

Anna

Anna and her mother hurried to greet their guest. As always, her mom's best friend had arrived in a carriage with two men who waited while she visited. Freya had explained to Anna once that she felt safer traveling with trusted drivers, since she didn't have her husband or her daughter accompanying her.

The pair watched as the first driver helped the woman in a dark hooded cape out of the carriage. She quickly walked inside the bakery and shut the door, removing her hood.

"Tomally!" Freya said warmly, embracing her friend. The two always hugged for so long when they saw each other Anna worried she'd never get a turn.

Anna's mother had told her that when Anna was adopted as a baby, Freya was the first one she'd called to come see her. Anna and Freya had spent so much time together over the years that Anna considered her an aunt. She couldn't imagine life without her.

Freya and Tomally finally parted, and Freya looked at Anna, her face warm with emotion. "Anna," she said softly, and opened her arms.

Freya always smelled sweet, like purple heather. Anna ran into her arms and squeezed. She was a hugger. She couldn't help it. "It's so good to see you!"

Freya stepped back, holding Anna by the shoulders, and looked at her intently. "Have you gotten taller? Tomally, is she taller? She's definitely taller!"

"I'm not taller," Anna said, and they all laughed. "I was the same height two months ago. *I think.*"

"You look bigger," Freya decided. She hung her cape by the door and removed her bonnet, revealing her beautiful dark brown hair. Anna always loved her dresses. The one she wore that day was dark green with yellow-and-blue trim and embroidered red flowers. Anna wondered if Freya had made it herself. She was a seamstress and always brought Anna new gowns. "Or maybe it's just that you're getting older."

"I am fifteen," Anna admitted.

Freya smiled softly. "That must be it. You're becoming a young woman." She looked at Tomally. "You've done a fine job raising her."

Tomally took Freya's hand and they looked at each other fondly. "It's been my honor. She's been the most wondrous gift."

"Ma." Anna rolled her eyes. She hated when her mother got all emotional like that. She and Freya always cried at some point when they got together.

"Sorry, sorry." Tomally busied herself at the table. "You must be hungry. Anna wanted to make you breakfast."

"I want to make you breakfast, too," Anna said to her mother. "They get too busy to eat," she told Freya, who sat down at the table alongside Tomally as Anna heated up a pan and cracked eggs into it for a quick scramble.

"How is business? Good, I hope?" Freya asked.

"We love it, but it has grown, thanks to some of Anna's specialties, and the orders have, too."

"And how is your tutoring going, Anna?" Freya asked.

"It's fine," Anna said with a sigh, moving the eggs around the pan. "I prefer when school is in session, because I like seeing people. Doing my studies with Ma is not as fun. No offense."

Freya and Tomally exchanged small smiles. "Well, that may be, but your studies are important, especially history and science."

Freya always wanted to make sure Anna was applying herself, which was sweet, but what Anna really wanted to hear about was *her* life. "So tell us what's going on down the mountain. How is Arendelle? Are there any festivals going on or parties to attend? Do you ever see the king and the queen when you're in the castle? Or the princess?"

Freya's face froze, and Anna wondered what she'd said wrong.

Tomally patted Anna's hand. "I think your aunt has had a long journey. Maybe we could save the questions for later. Let's have breakfast, then bake, shall we?"

Anna nodded.

A short while later, they were all covered in flour.

"Anna, do you have to use so much flour?" her mother asked, waving a cloud of dust away from her face.

"I hate when the cookies stick, Ma, you know that." Anna sifted more flour onto the wooden table that doubled as a workspace. She loved flour and she used it liberally, but it did make cleanup much harder.

The bakery wasn't large and it wasn't bright; the windows were high up, just below the ceiling eaves. Anna had to squint to see her measurements. Spoons and pots hung on the walls, and the large wooden table stood in the middle of the room, where Anna and her mom baked bread, cinnamon rolls, and Anna's famous cookies. The majority of the bakery was taken up by the cast-iron stove. It was as beautiful as it was functional, and Anna was constantly tripping over it—or falling into it, hence the small burn marks on her forearms. Those also came from paddling the bread into and out of the oven. Her parents said she was the best at knowing when the temperature of the stove was just right for baking the softest bread. Maybe she was a little messy when she baked, but it didn't bother her. She lifted her sifter again, and flour flew through the air, making Freya sneeze. "Sorry!"

"Don't apologize," said her aunt as she pulled out her handkerchief. Anna noticed it had the Arendelle crest embroidered on it.

Anna dropped a large ball of dough onto the table, then took another fistful of flour. "I just love to watch flour fall. It reminds me of snow."

Freya's blue eyes dimmed. "Do you like the snow?"

Anna patted the flour onto the dough, then used her rolling pin to flatten it. "I do! We get a lot of it up here in the mountains, obviously, and I've always been fond of ice-skating, playing in the snow, and making a good snowman."

"Of all your cookies, this has always been my favorite," her aunt said, staring fondly at the tin snowman cutters on the table. "When did you start making the snowmen? Last year?"

"Yes." Anna held up a cookie cutter. "I feel like I know him. Not *know him* know him, but I've seen him before."

"How so?" Freya asked.

The snowman in her mind's eye always had a large

bottom, a smaller middle snowball section, and an oval head, with two twig arms. She liked him to have a carrot nose and three coal buttons, with royal frosting. He looked happy and friendly. "I see him in my dreams. I kept drawing him over and over again, so finally Papa said he'd make me a cookie cutter that resembled him. I make so many cookies now that Papa's had to make dozens of cutters. We sold out of the cookies yesterday. Who knew this many people liked snowmen in the summer?"

Her aunt smiled. "I'm happy to help you make more cookies. I enjoy watching you work. Your mother is right— you're a wonderful baker."

"Anna created the recipe for this dough herself," her mother said proudly.

"Did you?" Freya asked.

Anna nodded. "I like to experiment. I've picked up my mother's love of baking."

"I see that." Freya watched Anna carefully use a knife to lift the snowmen off the table and place them on a baking sheet.

Anna looked up. "You never told me how everyone liked the sirupskake."

"It was splendid!" she said, her smile returning. "Your fa—*my husband* asked that you bake another one soon for me to bring him."

Freya was always tripping over her words like that. Anna did the same thing herself. She chalked it up to wanting to say so much in a short amount of time. She was like a pot of melting chocolate: the words bubbled over.

"Did he like the candied oranges I placed on top?"

"Yes! He said he'd never seen it done that way before."

Anna shrugged. "I love to put my own spin on recipes. I like to be unique, if you haven't noticed."

"I have." Freya smiled. "I think my husband would enjoy meeting you. You and I have a similar joyful spirit, while he"—she sighed—"carries the weight of the world on his shoulders, I'm afraid. Much like my daughter."

Freya talked about her daughter a lot but unfortunately never brought her along for visits. From what Anna knew, the girl seemed whip smart and serious. Anna wished she could meet her so she could shake her up a bit. Everyone needed to let their hair down sometimes. Plus it would be nice to have a friend close to her own age.

The clock in the kitchen chimed and Anna looked up. The first batch of cookies would be ready any moment; then it would be time to put in another tray. After that, there were four different types of bread, krumkaker (she wouldn't fill them with cream in this heat), and at least two spice cakes to make. Her mother hated the idea of her baking cakes that might not sell ("The ingredients cost money"), but Anna knew people would want them, and they made a tidy profit off cakes. It was a win-win.

"You must tell him not to worry so much," her mother said. "What is meant to be will be."

"I know. I'm sure he does as well, Tomally, but sometimes the future feels so far away," Freya said.

"Then focus on now," Anna said. "Right now you're doing something really fun with me."

Her aunt laughed. "That is true. We are blessed in so many ways."

Anna pulled the cookies out of the oven to let them cool. They were a light golden yellow, just how she liked them. She always timed them perfectly.

"Speaking of food, I almost forgot . . ." Freya dug into the woven basket she had brought and unwrapped the parchment paper. Inside was just what Anna wanted: several blocks of the darkest, thickest chocolate she'd ever seen.

Anna lifted one to her nose. The chocolate smelled divine. "Thank you! I promise I'll make this batch last till your next visit. Maybe."

"Fair enough." Freya laughed. "I may even be able to bring you some chocolate from another kingdom. My husband and I will be traveling the next few weeks."

"Traveling?" Anna's eyes lit up as she placed another tray of cookies in the oven. "Where are you going? How are you getting there? Are you bringing your daughter? Does she like to travel, too? What are you wearing?"

Freya started to laugh again. "So many questions!"

Anna's mother shook her head. "Always. The girl never stops talking."

Anna smiled. "I can't help myself."

"We're going alone, and our daughter is staying home with . . . help," Freya said, struggling to find the right words. "The journey is long, and it will be good to have someone stay back and take care of our affairs. She's older than you by three years, so she's practically an adult."

Anna began to prepare the icing by beating egg whites and powdered sugar. "I've never traveled before. I've never even been off this mountain."

"I know," Freya said thoughtfully. She looked at Anna's mother. "It would be wonderful if you could finally visit Arendelle."

Anna dropped her spoon into the icing with a loud thud. "Could I? I'd bring cookies. Which are your daughter's favorites? The snowmen? Your husband likes the spice cake, I know. . . ."

Her mother jumped in. "Anna, slow down."

Freya was quiet for a moment, lost in her own thoughts. "If I could finally find a way for you to visit, would you like to come stay with me?" Freya asked, her voice cracking.

"*Like* to come? Of course I'd like to come!" Anna squealed in delight.

Her mother smiled sadly at Freya. "Anna's always wanted to visit Arendelle. Do you think there is any way to make that sort of trip possible?"

"We don't know unless we ask," Freya said to Anna's mother. Then she looked at Anna. "You've waited long enough."

It was like they were speaking in code. They weren't making sense to her. It was just a trip to the kingdom. Why were they so hesitant? Anna wanted to ice the cookies fast so she could focus on the conversation. Quickly, she tested the icing on the first snowman, letting it drip from her spoon onto the cookie, then watched it spread out and drip over the sides, covering the snowman in white. She did several more snowmen, then put down the icing and spoke up.

"I want to visit Aunt Freya in Arendelle so badly," Anna said. She didn't want to hurt her parents, but she knew staying in Harmon wasn't her future. "Can I go? Please, Ma?"

Her mother sighed and looked at Freya. "We're so busy with the bakery we couldn't afford to have you gone for long." She paused. "But I'll talk to your father. It's not a guarantee," she stressed, "but I'll ask. You are bound to wind up there eventually."

"I've always wanted to meet your daughter," Anna said to Freya. "It would be nice to bake with someone my own age. No offense." Freya and Anna's mom laughed.

"Someday soon you two will be together," Freya said. "Your meeting is long overdue."

Arendelle. Anna could almost imagine the kingdom she'd spent so many years looking at from a distance. She'd see more than the tops of the turrets. She'd be right there in the middle of everything, with Freya, who knew the place so well. "Do you think Papa will say yes?" Anna asked her mother.

"Perhaps," Ma replied.

Freya smiled and took Anna's hand. She seemed hopeful. "When I get back from my trip, we will find a way to bring you to Arendelle."

CHAPTER SIX

Elsa

I might die of boredom.

Elsa would never say those words out loud, of course. But as she sat in the portrait hall in a large velvet chair and stared up at the ceiling, she couldn't help thinking them. Her parents had been gone only a week, but already she was feeling the weight of their absence. She'd done all her studies for the next three days, sat in on the visits her father had outlined for her, walked around the courtyard daily, and visited with Olina in the kitchen. The castle's chef was the closest thing she had to a real friend, if she was being honest. Miss Olina—who insisted Elsa call her Olina now that she was practically an adult—didn't care that she was the future queen of Arendelle. She gave it to Elsa straight.

"You need friends—or better yet, a suitor," she had told Elsa that morning. Elsa was sitting in the kitchen with her, eating eggs for breakfast.

Elsa groaned. "Now you sound like the Duke of Weselton." She knew where the conversation was headed: she was about to get a lecture.

"Would it be so wrong for you to find someone who is your equal?" Olina asked.

Elsa sighed deeply.

"You listen, my darling girl." Olina waved a wooden spoon, the pink in her cheeks from the heat of the stove growing deeper as she got wound up. "You spend too much time alone."

"But—" Elsa said, but Olina cut her off.

"I know you're learning how to follow in your father's footsteps, and that's good, but when was the last time you went outside the castle walls? With someone other than this staff? A good queen knows herself inside and out, and you are too inside your head. The only way you can understand the people you serve is to get to know them. Enjoy their company. Hear their stories. In the process you might figure out what you enjoy, as well, when you're not focused on your studies and your future."

Olina made a good point. What *did* Elsa enjoy doing other than spending time with her parents and learning how to be a wise ruler? Olina was right. She needed friends. She needed a hobby. She needed something to do. But what?

"Oh my goodness!" Olina said, spying Kai coming through the door with a large box. Various scrolls and hats were falling out of it. Olina ran over to help him place the box on the floor. "Let me help you with that."

"Thanks," Kai said. "That was heavier than I anticipated." He noticed Elsa. "Hello, Princess."

"Hello." Elsa nodded.

"Who told you to carry it all the way from the attic by yourself?" Olina scolded him, stepping back to the stove and stirring the contents of a large pot. Whatever she was cooking smelled wonderful. "How is it going in the attic?"

"Good. We cleared out several boxes. You can see the floor again now."

"You didn't throw out anything the king or queen would want, did you?" Olina asked, placing her hands on her hips.

"No, no, just these random old hats and broken things." Kai held up a Viking hat with one horn and a chipped blue vase. "Thought you might like this." He pulled out a large pot.

Olina's eyes lit up. "Look at that! I could put this to good use."

"I'll go up to the attic again tomorrow when it isn't so hot and see what else there is. I'll bring you back anything special. Good afternoon, Princess Elsa." Kai lifted the box again and walked out.

"Good afternoon," Elsa said.

She'd never realized there were things stored in the attic. She'd never even been up there. She had a whole afternoon ahead of her. Maybe it wouldn't hurt to have a peek at what was stored right above her bedroom. It wasn't a hobby, but it was a start.

After saying goodbye to Olina, Elsa decided to stop in her room to grab a lantern. With her parents away and no engagements being held at the castle until their return, it seemed like everyone was trying to catch up on long-overdue chores. She passed workers cleaning brass fixtures in the hallway and someone delicately brushing dust off their family portrait, painted when Elsa was eight. Finally, Elsa began to ascend the attic stairs, the heat rising as she climbed.

The lantern washed over the dark, cramped space. The room was musty, as if it hadn't been visited in centuries, even though Kai had just been there. Elsa could make out dust marks on the floor from the boxes Kai had taken downstairs. The space needed a good cleaning. Furniture was piled in one corner, a sled hung from another, and the tight quarters were crammed with massive trunks with chipped paint and faded rosemaling. Elsa made her way to the closest trunk to have a peek. It was locked. The next one contained nothing but quilts. The third was full of old hats and a few capes. The fourth one was also locked, but the mechanism was loose, so Elsa gave it a hard pull, and it came right off. The trunk was full of boring ice axes, fur-trimmed gloves, and snow boots that looked like they had been used to climb the North Mountain. She could see why Kai was emptying out the place. The excursion had been a waste of her time. There was nothing to see up there. Or was there?

Her father had lived in the castle since he was a boy, and she'd hate to see his childhood things tossed out by accident. After all, this was their history. She needed to protect it. Elsa stepped around one of the trunks, and she waved the lantern into the dark recesses. The light caught on a broken frame with a yellowed map of the kingdom. Her father might like to see that. She stepped close, her eyes lingering on handwritten markings, and lifted the frame up to the dim light. That was when she noticed there was a trunk behind the frame. This one was different from the others. It was painted white, with brightly colored flowers on the front of it. Elsa realized immediately why it seemed familiar: it looked exactly like her hope chest.

Could it have been her mother's, before she married?

Elsa ran her hand along the top of the trunk, removing a thick layer of dust. The painted markings on it were identical to the ones on her own, but instead of an *E* painted on top, the tracings of a different letter were buried under all that dust. She rubbed hard at the spot, wiping the dust away until the letter became clear. It was an *A*.

A? Her mother's name was Iduna. Her father was Agnarr, but this clearly wasn't his. Who was A?

Elsa racked her brain, trying to think of who the trunk could belong to. A name was rolling around in her head, but it wouldn't come forward. *A . . . A . . . A . . .* She willed her mind to figure it out, but it was stuck.

Instead, she thought again about that argument she had overheard between her parents. They had referred to a "she." Her mother had seemed insistent on seeing the person, while her father kept stressing how risky it was to visit. She'd never heard them that upset with each other before. Now she wondered: could "she" and "A" be the same person?

"Princess Elsa!"

She stepped away from the trunk as if she had been caught snooping.

"Princess Elsa!"

She quickly put the frame back where she had found it, hiding the chest from sight, and headed down the stairs. There was a commotion of some sort. She could hear people crying and others calling her name.

"I'm here," Elsa called, instantly feeling guilty for making anyone worry about where she was. She rounded the corner and found members of the castle staff gathered together. Gerda was inconsolable. Olina was crying into a handkerchief. Several people were embracing and in tears.

"Princess Elsa!" Kai clutched his chest. "You're all right." His face was blotchy, as if he'd been crying, too. "We thought . . ."

"Thought what?" Elsa felt her heart speed up. A lump rose in her throat as she watched Olina blot her eyes. Everyone was looking at her. Something was terribly wrong. "What is it?"

Lord Peterssen appeared from the middle of the crowd. His face was somber and his eyes were bloodshot. "Elsa," he whispered, her name sounding broken on his tongue, "could we speak in private, please?"

The minute she locked eyes with him, she knew.

"No." She started to back up. She didn't want to hear what he had to say. The walls seemed like they were closing in on her. The crying and the sobbing grew louder. She felt her heart racing. Her mouth was dry and there was a ringing in her ears. She knew what he would tell her would change her life forever, and for just a moment, she wanted to stall him. "I don't want to speak in private. I want to stay here with everyone."

Gerda put her arm around Elsa, steadying her.

Lord Peterssen looked around, his eyes wet. "All right. Elsa, there is no easy way to say this."

She inhaled sharply. *Then don't,* she wanted to shout.

"Your parents' ship didn't make it to the port." His voice faltered.

"Maybe it's gone off course." Elsa felt her fingertips starting to tingle. It was a strange sensation. She pulled away from Gerda and shook them out. "Send a ship to find them."

He shook his head. "We already have. We sought word from every nearby port, every kingdom. Now we have received responses from them all: the ship never arrived. Moreover, the Southern Seas can be treacherous, and there have been many storms lately." He paused. "There is only one conclusion left to draw."

"*No.*" Elsa's voice was rougher now. Gerda immediately burst into tears again. "That can't be!"

Lord Peterssen swallowed hard, and she watched his Adam's apple move up and down. His lip quivered and Olina let out an audible sob. Several of the others bowed their heads. She heard Kai praying. "Elsa, King Agnarr and Queen Iduna are gone."

"May their souls rest in peace," said Olina, closing her eyes and tilting her face to the heavens. Others did the same.

"No," Elsa repeated. Her whole body began to shake. Her fingers began to tingle again. She had the sudden feeling she was about to burst into a million pieces, exploding in fragments of light. Lord Peterssen reached for her, but she backed away, trying to disappear. Kai held up a thin piece of black silk. He and Gerda hung it over the portrait of her parents in the hallway.

Her parents couldn't be . . . dead. They were her only family. Without them, she truly was alone. Her breath became ragged and her heart beat so fast she thought it would leap out of her chest. Every sound she heard was magnified a thousand times. *"No!"* Her fingers were burning now. *"No!"* She turned and ran, not stopping till she reached her room.

Elsa fell through the doors with such force they slammed shut behind her. She landed on the circular rug and didn't have the strength to move. Instead, she curled up into a ball and stared at the pink wallpaper where a portrait of her as a child stared back at her. That girl was smiling and happy. She had a family.

Now she had none.

The burning sensation in her fingers was growing stronger, her heart pulsing so fast she felt like she could hear it. Tears began to stream down her face, wetting the top of her collar and reaching her hot chest. Shaking, Elsa forced herself to stand up, looking for someone—anyone—to talk to. No one was there. She had closed herself off once again. Elsa went to her hope chest. Her hand shook as she brushed the green wooden lockbox under the quilt. She rummaged around until she found what she was looking for: the small one-eyed handmade penguin she had confided in as a girl—Sir JorgenBjorgen. She held the penguin with shaking hands, but couldn't put her thoughts into words. Mama and Papa were gone.

I might die of boredom. Wasn't that what she'd thought earlier that day? How could she have been so selfish? She clutched Sir JorgenBjorgen so tightly she felt like he might disintegrate in her burning hands. They started to shake so badly she couldn't hang on to him. She threw the doll across the room and he landed on her bed.

Alone. Alone. Alone.

Dead. Dead. Dead.

Gone. Gone. Gone.

She closed her eyes. She felt a scream rising inside her. It was so primal she knew it would rattle the whole castle, but she didn't care. It gurgled to the top of her throat, threatening to overtake her, until it finally did, and Elsa screamed so hard she thought she might never stop. Her hands went from hot to burning cold as they flew out in front of her. Something inside her opened, like a chasm that could never be closed again. Opening her eyes, she saw it, unbelievably, form in the air in front of her fingers.

Ice.

It shot clear across the room, hitting the opposite wall

and crawling up to the ceiling. Terrified and still sobbing, Elsa jumped back in fear as the ice continued to grow. It crackled as it moved under her feet, spreading along the floor till it climbed up the other walls, too.

What was happening?

The ice was coming from inside her. It didn't make sense, yet she knew it was true. She'd caused this to happen. What was happening?

Magic.

She'd heard Papa use that word when he and Mama had been arguing. Had they been talking about her?

Elsa sank down along the nearest wall, collapsing in grief.

Alone. Alone. Alone.

Gone. Gone. Gone.

More and more ice shot out as she choked back sobs. Was her heartbreak causing this? Had her parents known she was capable of such strange magic? Or was this something she had been born with and didn't know she possessed? She'd never been more frightened in her entire life. Without her parents, there was no one she trusted enough even to ask. She needed them now more than ever before.

She banged her head on the wall and closed her eyes. Her voice was barely a whisper. "Papa, Mama, please don't leave me here alone."

CHAPTER SEVEN

Anna

Anna couldn't remember the last time she'd crawled back into her bed when the sun was still shining. Papa and Ma had insisted she retire for a spell. She'd been up late the night before, assembling a traditional Arendelle wedding cake the Larsen family had paid her handsomely for. She rarely made that particular type of cake because it was so time-consuming—between the icing and all the layers that needed to be baked, it took hours—but the end result was worth it. Anna knew that the Larsens' daughter, who was getting married later today, was going to love it. So it was with a grateful, sleepy sigh that she pulled up her quilt, fluffed her pillow, and closed her eyes.

She couldn't fall asleep right away. Her mind wandered back to the cake. She pictured the Larsens raving about it to their guests. Guests who had traveled from Arendelle and would go back to the kingdom talking about Anna's work. Soon the king and queen would hear of her baking. Maybe they'd request she bake for them at the castle. Wouldn't her parents and Freya be proud? There was no way they'd hold her back from moving to Arendelle if they knew the king and queen were requesting her work. She could just see herself making snowman cookies for the royal family. The cookies immediately made her think of her aunt.

Anna hoped Freya would be back from her travels soon and that when she returned, she'd convince Ma and Papa to let Anna visit Arendelle. Her mother kept stressing that it wasn't a definite. "Freya works a great deal. We have to find the right time for you to go, if you can go at all." Her mother never stopped worrying! Neither did Papa. He talked about driving her down the mountain himself and waiting nearby in case she wanted to leave early. She couldn't remember the last time Papa had left Harmon. She tried convincing them that they should close the shop and all go together for a few days, but Papa wouldn't hear of it. "We don't even know if you will be able to go," he'd said. But Anna knew in her heart of hearts that Arendelle was in her future. She could feel it in every inch of her being.

When Anna finally drifted off, she didn't dream of snowmen. This dream was unpleasant. Anna felt cold, like she was sitting in a block of ice, and she couldn't see her hand in front of her face. Snow was swirling all around as if she were in a blizzard, but the weather didn't seem like a regular storm. It was filled with a darkness that threatened to swallow her whole. Even worse, she sensed that someone out there desperately needed her to find them.

Anna tried to fight the weather to get to them, turning into the pelting ice and wind to search, but she couldn't see the person. She could hear wailing, but it was so far in the distance she didn't know where it was coming from. All she knew was that she needed to find this person before it was too late. Something told her if she followed her heart and trusted her instincts, she would.

"Is anyone there?" Anna cried over the wind, but no one answered her. She had never felt more alone. She took a step forward and plunged off the edge of a snowy cliff.

Anna woke up gasping for air. "*Help!* She needs help!" She clutched her chest as if it hurt. "It was just a dream," she repeated over and over. But it hadn't felt like a dream. It felt real.

She needed to get out of that room.

Anna threw back the covers and slid into her shoes. The sun was lower in the sky than it had been earlier. Her parents would soon be finishing up for the day. Maybe a walk would do her good.

She slipped out the front door without saying goodbye and began to wander the village aimlessly. For once, she didn't stop and talk to every person she saw. Instead, she kept her head down and hugged her arms to her chest, trying to smother the cold that seemed to permeate her body. It was a dream, yet it had felt so real.

Someone had been in terrible pain, but all wasn't lost. If she trusted her instincts, Anna knew she could help. How strange . . .

She rubbed her arms to keep warm, walking aimlessly. Suddenly, a carriage roared down the road, startling her. Anna watched as it came to a halt in front of the church and a palace guard jumped out. Anna had never seen an official royal carriage in Harmon before. The guard nailed a proclamation to the church door, spoke to the bishop who came out to greet him, then got in the carriage and raced away. The bishop started talking to anyone who approached, and people began to run back to their homes with the news. Others flooded out of their houses, making their way to the proclamation to see what was written. Anna drifted closer and watched a woman read the news and gasp. Someone next to her burst into tears. There was commotion and wailing. Suddenly, the church bells began to toll. Anna tried to get through the crowd to see what was written, but people were pushing and shoving in an effort to get a closer look. Still she hugged her arms to her chest, struggling to get warm. It was silly, but she almost felt like she was still dreaming.

"Excuse me," Anna said to a man who had just been standing near the front steps. "Can you tell me what the guard posted on the church?"

He wiped his eyes. "The king and queen, rest their souls, have been lost at sea. Their ship never reached its destination."

"What?" Anna clutched her chest. "No!"

"Yes," he said, pushing farther into the crowd. "The proclamation says we are entering a period of mourning."

"And Princess Elsa?" Anna said, afraid to hear his response.

"She lives," he said. "Spread the word and pray for Arendelle and our future queen. She is on her own now."

I must tell Ma and Papa, Anna thought. She ran all the way to the bakery and found Papa sweeping the shop floor. When she flew through the door, slamming it behind her, he looked up, startled.

"What's wrong?" Papa dropped the broom and moved toward her. "Anna Bear, are you all right? I heard the carriage. Someone said it was royal, but I didn't go out to see. Is something the matter?"

Anna nodded, trying hard not to cry. "Where is Ma?"

"Here." Ma came from the entry to their house, wiping her hands on her apron. She, too, saw Anna's face, and her own fell. "What's the matter?"

"I think you should both sit down," Anna said. "Come into the living room."

Her parents followed her inside, but they wouldn't sit. They were holding hands. Anna took a deep breath. "There's been a terrible tragedy. The king and queen have been lost at sea." She closed her eyes; the news was almost too much even to think about.

"No!" her mother wailed so loud Anna began to shake. "That's impossible! What happened?"

Anna's lower lip trembled. "The castle just posted a proclamation. We are to enter a period of mourning. The king and queen's ship never made it to its destination." She bowed her head. "King Agnarr and Queen Iduna, may they rest in peace." It was so tragic she couldn't bear it, and both her parents were inconsolable. Her mother fell into a chair in a heap while her father rocked back and forth.

"No, why? *Why?*" he called to the heavens.

Anna tried to comfort her mother. "It's terrible, I know. But all is not lost. The princess is safe. We will have a queen again."

Her mother cried harder. Papa put his arm around Anna.

"When she turns twenty-one, she will take their place at the throne. But for now . . ."

"That poor girl," Anna whispered. She imagined her all alone in that big castle. She rubbed her chest. She couldn't get warm. "I can't believe the princess lost her parents."

There was silence in the room. Finally, Papa spoke. "Tomally, we must tell her," he said.

Anna looked from her mother to her father. "Tell me what?"

"Yes," her mother agreed, and reached for Anna's hands. "There is something you don't know." She sighed heavily. "Anna Bear, the queen had several ladies of the court with her on the ship. One of those ladies was Freya." Ma burst into tears again, and Papa put his arm around her shoulders.

"Freya? No! Freya?" Anna immediately started to cry. "Are you sure? What about her family? Were they with her?"

Ma looked at Papa. "Her husband would be lost as well, but Freya told us their daughter was staying home."

"Should we send for her? Does she have other family?" Anna whispered, her grief overwhelming her. "Will she be all right?"

"She will be fine," Ma said, but she couldn't stop crying.

"Papa, this can't be true, can it? Are you sure Freya was on that ship?" Anna asked.

Her father hesitated. "Yes." His jaw shook. "This was

the trip Freya spoke of on her last visit. She didn't like to boast, but she traveled with the king and queen." His eyes filled with tears. "Our dear friend is gone."

Yes, Anna was sad the king and queen had perished, but Freya was family. Anna felt weak in the knees. Her father reached out with his free arm to steady her. She sank to the floor, reaching for her mother to comfort her. "Not Freya. No!" She buried her head in her mother's chest.

Her mother stroked her hair. "Anna Bear, I'm so sorry. So terribly sorry," she choked out. She pulled her daughter away from her so she could look her in the eyes. "There's something else you should know, too."

"Tomally!" Papa's voice was sharp. "You made a vow. You cannot break it now."

Anna winced. She'd never heard her father raise his voice to her mother before.

"I have to, Johan! She deserves to know the truth! If not now, when?"

"It's not your truth to tell!" he argued.

What truth? "I'm fifteen. If there is more, I want to hear it."

Ma smiled sadly. "Nothing, darling. I'm sorry. I'm just terribly upset. Freya was my oldest and dearest friend."

Anna reached for her mother again, and they clung to each other. Papa put an arm around each of them.

They were grieving; it made sense their emotions were high. She could feel the tears coming harder now. Freya wasn't coming back. Their king and queen were gone. The walls seemed like they were closing in, but Anna refused to let them.

Her eyes searched for a comforting sight. Over her mother's shoulder, she found the living room window. The image was hard to see with her eyes filled with tears, but Anna knew it was there. If she peered out between two rows of houses and looked toward the bottom of the mountain, Arendelle was still there, calling for her. She couldn't help wondering what was happening inside the castle walls at that very moment. Who was comforting Princess Elsa?

Anna clung tighter to her parents. More than anything, Anna hoped Elsa wasn't alone.

CHAPTER EIGHT

Elsa

Elsa stared up at the ice-covered ceiling while snow fell around her.

It had been three days since she had learned her parents' ship was lost at sea. She hadn't left her room. She didn't sleep in her bed. She hardly touched the food left outside her door. She refused to see anyone, including Lord Peterssen, who was the closest thing she had left to family. All she wanted was to be left alone.

Snowflakes fell onto her nose and cheeks as she stared at the icicles hanging from the ceiling. Icicles she had somehow created.

How ironic that she had been given these strange powers at the exact moment she no longer had anyone to share them with.

She lifted her hand, fingers trembling, and felt the ice slipping loose again. The ice formed a frosty path across the ceiling. Elsa still wasn't sure how it worked, but at least she could sense when it was about to happen now. She would feel tingling in her fingers and her heart would speed up. She noticed it always happened when she was thinking about her parents. Did she even think about anything else now? No.

She was not getting up off the floor anytime soon.

There was a quiet knock at the door. She knew who it was without asking.

"I am leaving soon for the memorial. Please consider coming with me, Elsa."

It was Lord Peterssen. Even though she hadn't left her room, she knew what he was talking about. Kai, Gerda, Olina, and Lord Peterssen had been talking to her through her closed door for days.

Nothing they could tell her was of importance. She already knew who would run the kingdom. Papa had told her before his trip that if anything ever happened to him, Lord Peterssen would handle affairs until Elsa came of age at twenty-one and could be coronated. Anything else they had to say didn't matter.

It upset her to think she didn't know her parents as well as she had thought she did. When she considered the argument she had overheard before they left, the trunk in the attic with the mysterious letter *A*, and her strange powers, she had to wonder. There were so many questions she wished she could ask her parents. *Did you know I was capable of magic? If you did, why didn't you tell me? Were you ashamed I was born with this power? Scared? Worried about what our people would think? I'll never know. You've taken your secrets to the grave and left me alone to figure things out.*

"Elsa, please? Your parents would want you to be there. Open the door."

She closed her eyes tight. The memorial service for her parents was being held high above the fjord. Even though Papa and Mama had perished at sea, markers were being placed up there in their honor. Hundreds of subjects were expected to turn out. They'd want to offer their condolences and sympathy, but she knew she wouldn't be able to handle the situation. Ice would shoot out uncontrollably. They'd brand her a witch or a monster. They'd demand she abdicate the throne. Her parents' legacy would be gone in a moment.

No, she couldn't go to her parents' memorial. She couldn't go anywhere in public till she got a handle on her magic.

Until then, she would stay locked in her room. She'd never leave the castle. She would avoid contact with most of the staff. Her sole purpose would be to conceal her powers. *Don't feel it,* she reminded herself. *Don't let it show.*

Her parents had loved her so much. She still needed them—she was desperate to tell them what had happened. What if she couldn't handle the power on her own? She couldn't tell Lord Peterssen for fear of frightening him. The throne was at stake. She had no choice but to suffer in silence.

"Elsa? Can you hear me?"

"What is she saying?" said a second voice, much more insistent than the first.

Elsa heard Lord Peterssen patiently trying to explain the situation.

"I know she's upset," said the second voice, "but it won't look right for the future queen not to be at her parents' memorial. What will the people think?"

It was cleary the Duke of Weselton. He had no say in their kingdom, but he seemed to feel that being a close trade partner allowed him to weigh in on things. He had raced back to Arendelle when news broke of the king's and queen's demises. As much as his presence frustrated her, she knew he was right. She should honor her parents and be at the service. But that would mean she'd have to pick herself up off the floor and risk everyone's finding out what she was capable of.

"Please leave," Elsa croaked.

Silence.

"She isn't coming," Elsa heard Lord Peterssen tell the Duke. He didn't argue. Moments later, she heard them walk away.

Elsa sat up and looked at Sir JorgenBjorgen lying on her bed. He had been there since she'd thrown him days before. Now he was covered in ice. She suddenly wished she could reach him. When she was a child, she had truly loved that toy. Not just because the doll had been such a good listener, but because he was her constant companion. She had liked to imagine that the doll loved her in return.

For a split second, Elsa recalled a new memory of her younger self. She was building a snowman with another girl. They pulled the snowman around the room laughing. It was clear they loved each other. Her hands started to tingle in an unfamiliar way—they were warm—then the sensation was gone and she was left with a sharp headache.

What was that? she wondered. The girl had to be in her imagination. She had never used magic before that week. Had she?

Elsa stood up, her legs shaking. She held on to her bed frame to keep from falling. Heart pounding, fingers aching, she closed her eyes again and tried to remember the love she had just felt coursing through her veins. The emotion was stronger than fear. This feeling had come from building something out of love—a snowman for the two girls to enjoy.

If only she could capture that in a bottle and hold it close. Especially now, when she was more alone than she ever had been before.

It couldn't hurt to try.

Swirling her arms right and left, Elsa allowed the ice and snow to burst forth, but this time, she tried to focus on the love and leave the fear out of it. She thought again of the vision of her and the girl laughing and building a snowman. When she opened her eyes, the snow was swirling like a cyclone in front of her. It funneled up from the ground, creating snowballs that were pulled into the air and formed into a snowman. He had a wide bottom and two stubby snowball feet, a modest middle section, and an oval head with a large mouth and prominent front teeth. Elsa stumbled back in disbelief at her creation. Had she really just controlled her powers to build a snowman? She almost laughed at the absurdity of it. But Elsa pushed forward and focused on the snowman in front of her, grabbing kindling from the fire for his arms and hair, some coal from the ashes for buttons, and a carrot from last night's dinner plate for his nose. When she stepped back to admire her work, she noticed something strange. The snowman suddenly glowed with the same blue haze her powers had. When the glow faded, the snowman blinked his big eyes. Elsa jumped back in surprise.

"Hi! I'm Olaf, and I like warm hugs."

Wait, the snowman was *alive*? Her powers could do more than create snow—they could make a real being? Elsa's breath was shallow as she watched the snowman begin to walk—walk!—around her room. She stared at her hands in wonder. How was this even possible? "Did you just talk?" Elsa whispered, not believing her eyes or ears.

"Yes! I'm Olaf," the snowman repeated. He picked up Sir JorgenBjorgen. "Ooh! What's this? Hi," he said to her doll. "I'm Olaf!"

"Olaf," she repeated, trying to calm down. Why did the snowman's name sound so familiar?

"Elsa, you built me," the snowman said. "Remember?"

"You know who I am?"

"Yeah, why?" Olaf toddled away to examine the window seat.

Elsa was stunned by what was happening, but what was more, for a split second she'd forgotten her sorrow. A memory of love had led her to create a walking, talking snowman.

"Ooh! This room is pretty," Olaf said. "What's that?" he asked, moving to the open window and looking out below. Elsa watched him in awe. "Ooh! It's a village. I've always wanted to see a village with people and animals, and it's summertime! I love summer! Watching all the bees buzz around and kids blow dandelion fuzz and—oh." He turned toward her. The right side of his face was beginning to melt. "Small problem."

Elsa swirled her hands around as she had before and thought hard about what she could do to help him stay cool in the heat. A small snow cloud appeared above Olaf's head.

"My own personal flurry!" Olaf hugged himself. Then he saw the look on her face. "What's the matter?"

"I'm still trying to understand how you're here and how I created you."

"Don't you remember?" Olaf asked. "You made me for Anna!"

Elsa's heart might have stopped for a moment.

Anna?

Could Anna be the *A* on the chest in the attic?

Elsa was almost too afraid to ask. "Who's Anna?"

Olaf's eager smile faded. "I don't know. Who's Anna?"

It was okay. This was a start. She had a name now. "I don't know, either." Elsa took Olaf by the twig and led him to her window seat. She planned on telling him everything she knew. "But together we're going to find out."

CHAPTER NINE

Elsa

Three Years Later . . .

Elsa looked out her bedroom window and marveled at the scene unfolding in front of her. The castle gates were open and workers in green uniforms were readying the courtyard and the chapel for her coronation. Purple and gold banners, some with her silhouette and others with the family crest, were being hung from every flagpole inside and outside the courtyard. Her coronation was only days away.

Elsa was terrified.

She took a deep breath and tried to steady her heartbeat before the blue glow could appear above her hands. *Don't let them see your powers,* she reminded herself. *You need them to think of you as the good ruler your parents raised you to be, not someone who can do magic, or else . . .* She exhaled slowly and thought about the worst-case scenario: *One wrong move and everyone will know the truth. I'm not like everyone else.*

There was a knock at her door. "Princess Elsa? Your presence is requested in the dressing room for a final fitting of your gown."

It was Gerda calling her from the hallway. Elsa was thankful for her presence, as well as Kai's and Lord Peterssen's, the past three years. Her room had become her sanctuary after her parents' deaths, and they had respected that, allowing her to take the time she needed before she was ready to join the world again. She spent a lot of time in her room and the adjoining one that was her dressing area, but didn't like to linger in the castle's other rooms. She was still haunted by the memories of her parents.

"Thank you, Gerda. I'll meet you in the dressing room," Elsa called through the door.

Gerda understood her better than almost anyone, and yet she didn't know Elsa's secret. Only one person knew that.

"Oooh, look! You got more flowers!" said Olaf, walking through the door between her room and the dressing area with a large bouquet.

"Olaf!" Elsa pulled him through the door before Gerda saw him. "You know you're not supposed to be in the dressing room. You can't leave my room at all without me. Especially this week. There are too many people in the castle."

"Technically, I didn't leave your room," Olaf pointed out. "The dressing room is attached."

Elsa took the flowers from Olaf and placed them on her desk. "I know, but you promised me you'd stay in here."

The snowflakes over Olaf's head fell faster. "But it looks like so much fun out there! I peeked through the keyhole and saw someone pushing a cart with a chocolate cake."

"I will have some cake sent to the room," Elsa promised. "I know it's hard, but we can't risk anyone finding a talking snowman roaming the halls today."

Olaf frowned. "You say that every day."

She grabbed his twiglike hand. "I know. I'm sorry."

There were no words for how sorry she was. Olaf was the closest thing she had to family. He had been her constant companion the past three years, and she never let him leave the room unless she was absolutely positive they weren't going to be seen.

Occasionally, the two of them escaped her room. A few times she had stuck Olaf underneath a tea cart and wheeled him to the staircase so they could dash up to the attic. Repeated trips had turned up nothing on Anna. The mysterious trunk with the letter *A* held tiny dresses and bonnets, but there was nothing there that suggested *A* was for *Anna*, or that it was a clue to who Anna was. Elsa had exhausted herself searching for information on this lost girl Olaf was sure she knew. Visits to her parents' library also turned up nothing, and there was no record in the castle chapel of an Anna being born. Once, she'd even mentioned Anna's name to Lord Peterssen, hoping to get a reaction, but he looked utterly confused. The only one who remembered her was Olaf, and he apparently had memory loss.

"After the coronation, we will find time to let you poke around the attic again," Elsa said brightly, and Olaf's eyes widened.

"Not just the attic!" Olaf said. "Once you're queen you can tell everyone about your wonderful gift."

Gift. Sometimes the gift felt more like a curse. She'd learned to control her magic a bit in the past few years, but only when it came to what she could intentionally create. Snow mounds, yes. But if she found herself getting upset or anxious, she couldn't stop snow from falling, no matter how hard she tried. "I'm not sure that's wise."

"Why not? Everyone would love some snow on a day as hot as this." Olaf walked to the window, his personal flurry cloud following, and looked out. "They're roasting out there getting everything ready for your coronation. Oh, look! They have lots of banners for you. Hi, people!"

Elsa pulled him back from the window. "I am not sure

the kingdom will be happy to know they have a queen who can make ice."

"Anna always liked it," Olaf offered.

That was what he'd do sometimes. He'd drop Anna's name into the conversation as if they should both know who he was talking about. But the minute she tried to pull at the loose thread, the conversation unraveled.

"When did I make snow for Anna, again?"

Olaf clapped his hands excitedly. "Ooh . . . well . . ." He frowned. "I don't remember."

Elsa smiled sadly. "It's all right. One day you will."

Olaf nodded. "Let's see you practice for your coronation again."

"I'm not sure I'm ready to do that right now." Elsa hesitated. "Gerda is waiting."

"You can do it this time!" Olaf cheered her on. "I know you can."

"All right." Elsa walked to her desk and looked down at the small porcelain jar and candlestick. She had been using them as stand-ins for the orb and scepter she would have to hold, like her father did during his coronation. As she had many times before, Elsa closed her eyes and tried to imagine herself inside the chapel where the ceremony would take place. She thought of the choir that would be singing in the balcony, and she could see the pulpit she would be standing at in front of the priest and all her people, as well as nobles and visiting dignitaries. With no family, she'd be up there alone. Elsa tried not to think about that as she imagined the priest placing the jeweled tiara on her head. Then he'd hold out the pillow with the orb and scepter for her to take. She couldn't wear her teal gloves during that portion of the ceremony, so she removed them now for practice. She wore gloves all the time these days. Perhaps it was silly, but she thought the gloves helped her conceal her magic. This was her battle cry: Conceal it. Don't feel it. Don't let it show.

"You're almost there," Olaf said encouragingly.

This was the hardest part. Elsa reached down with trembling fingers and lifted the porcelain jar in one hand and the candlestick in the other. She repeated the prayer she knew the priest would say while she held the objects. *"Sem hón heldr inum helgum eignum ok krýnd í þessum helga stað ek té fram fyrir yðr* . . . Queen Elsa of Arendelle."

Then she would need to turn around with the orb and scepter in her hands as the people chanted, "Queen Elsa of Arendelle!"

"Queen Elsa of Arendelle!" Olaf shouted.

Elsa held her breath. *I can do this. I can do this. I can do this,* she told herself. Her hands trembled despite her attempts to keep them steady. Olaf watched her anxiously. *I can do this.*

The bottom of the porcelain jar began to crackle with ice. The candlestick froze in her fingers. She quickly put them down and pulled on her gloves.

"You almost had it." Olaf smiled toothily. "We'll try again later."

She couldn't tell Olaf it was hopeless. How would she get through the ceremony without giving herself away?

But Olaf had already moved on. "Look at your beautiful flowers!" Olaf said. "Don't they smell great?" He took a whiff and sneezed all over them. "I wonder who they're from?"

Elsa picked up the card that was tucked inside the bouquet of purple heather. "I have a pretty good idea." She read the note.

I enjoyed spending time with you yesterday. Could I entice you with another walk around the garden this afternoon? I think it will help put your mind at ease about your big day.

Elsa smiled to herself.

"The prince really does like you!" Olaf observed, looking over her shoulder. "I think."

"Perhaps," she agreed.

"He's asked you for a walk every day since he arrived!" Olaf reminded her. "And he's sent you chocolates, flowers, and all those books."

"That's true." The prince was always talking to her about

the books he read—he loved to read as much as she did—and whenever he finished another one, he had it delivered to her room with a single flower pressed inside the pages.

The prince had accompanied the Duke of Weselton on a trip to Arendelle a few months earlier, and she'd been surprised at how well she and he had hit it off. Unlike the nosy duke, the prince was polite and seemed to know she needed time to warm up to people. He asked thoughtful questions about her studies and training and liked to discuss history and architecture. They'd spent hours talking about her family's rule in Arendelle and how it had lasted several decades. His family was relatively new to the throne in his kingdom, so he constantly wanted to hear her opinions on trade and foreign affairs. They'd become so close, yet there was still so much she couldn't tell him.

There was another knock on the dressing room door. "Elsa? Are you ready?"

"Coming!" Elsa called. She looked back at Olaf.

"I know what to do," he told her. "Stay here, be quiet, and if anyone appears, hide. Maybe I'll even do some cleaning. This room is rather dusty."

He wasn't wrong. Since she never let anyone in to clean, it had gotten a bit musty. "Good idea. If you get bored, maybe you can see if there is anything in my hope chest I don't need anymore," she said. "I don't think I've looked in there for years."

Olaf nodded. "Ooh! I love hope chests." He headed off to the chest and opened it wide. "Wow! There's lots crammed in here."

Elsa left him with his project. She came through the doorway between her dressing area and her bedroom and found Gerda patiently waiting. She stood next to a dress form, holding the gown Elsa would wear for her coronation. Every detail had been carefully planned for her big day.

Gerda smiled. "This is a gown fit for a queen, is it not?"

Elsa returned the smile. She didn't have the heart to tell Gerda she found the dress a bit heavy when she walked, and the high neckline was restricting. Every time she put the gown on, she felt claustrophobic. "Everything you bring in is beautiful, Gerda." This small room was one of her favorites. She loved the soothing blue hues of the wallpaper and the white wood accents, hand-painted with gold and purple rosemaling that picked up the colors of the rug on the floor. Sometimes she still couldn't believe that she had a whole room just for dressing, but it helped to know she could walk into the adjacent room and not have to hide Olaf away.

"Shall we do one last fitting?" Gerda asked.

Elsa obliged, slipping behind the screen to put on the gown. When she emerged, Gerda had her stand on a wooden box in front of the large trifold mirror so that they could make final alterations.

There was a knock at the dressing room door. "May I enter?"

"Yes," Gerda and Elsa said at the same time.

Lord Peterssen looked as if he might cry when he saw her. "Elsa, you are lovely. If your parents could see you today . . ."

She touched his hand. "I know. They'd be proud."

He pulled a handkerchief out of the pocket of his blue jacket. "They truly would be. As am I," he said with a smile.

The past three years had aged him. His thick black hair had thinned, and the gray was seeping through. He looked tired all the time. She could relate. Her parents' absence had weighed on them both. But now the day had come when he would step aside from handling the royal affairs, while she would be entering a lifetime of duty. How was she going to keep her secret safe from the kingdom?

She felt her fingertips beginning to tingle inside her gloves. She pulled her hand away from Gerda, who was fixing a stitch on the gown's midsection.

"This gown is ready and so are you," Gerda said reassuringly.

A crash came from the other side of her bedroom wall. Then she heard a loud shriek.

Lord Peterssen appeared baffled. "Is there someone inside your chamber?"

Elsa stepped off the box and began backing out of the room. "Please excuse me for one moment. I left my windows open. A bird must have flown in," she said. *What is Olaf doing?* "I'll take care of it."

"Do you want help?" Gerda asked.

"No!" Elsa said, a bit more forcefully than she intended. "I'll be right back."

Elsa hurried through the door to her bedroom and closed it. When she turned around, she saw Olaf had emptied her entire trunk. Papers, gowns, trinkets, and mementos were scattered around the floor. Olaf was bent over an object she couldn't see, and he groaned loudly as he tried to lift it.

"Olaf!" she whispered. "What are you—oh!"

Olaf stood over a green wooden box she had long forgotten about. It was the lockbox her father had given her right before his final journey. Seeing it again brought tears to her eyes. "I forgot about this," she said.

"Is it a present?" Olaf asked. "It's so heavy!"

"It's kind of like a present," Elsa said, her heart warming at the sight of the rosemaling on the lid. She fingered the raised gold crest on the top. "My father used one of these boxes as king, and he gave me this one to have when I ruled. I guess that time is now."

"What's inside?" Olaf asked excitedly.

It was the first time in years she had opened the box. She lifted the lid and the empty green velvet lining stared back at them.

"It's empty." Olaf frowned.

"Elsa?" she heard from the dressing room.

"Coming!" Elsa placed the lockbox on the desk. "Thank you for finding this. I'll return soon," Elsa told him before slipping back into the dressing room, where Gerda was waiting patiently. "Bird. It's gone now," she explained.

"Why don't you change and I'll hang up the gown?" Gerda suggested. "Lord Peterssen had to leave, but you have another visitor waiting outside."

Elsa quickly went behind the screen to change. Olaf would be okay in her room for a spell. It was a lovely day, and a walk around the castle grounds could be just what she needed. When she was dressed and ready, Gerda opened the door so Elsa could greet her guest. She had a feeling she knew who it was.

He bowed. "Princess Elsa of Arendelle, thank you for seeing me." He held out his bent elbow. "Shall we take a walk?"

She took his arm. "Prince Hans of the Southern Isles, I'd be delighted."

CHAPTER TEN

Hans

"You do not need to bow every time you see me, Hans," Elsa said with a laugh.

He flashed her a charming smile and sighed. "Force of habit. I'll stop doing that with time."

Over the past few months, he'd given Elsa *a lot* of time.

He'd been patient.

He'd been a good listener.

He moved slowly, each motion or statement he made carefully considered. Hans learned quickly that the princess of Arendelle required a delicate approach.

The poor thing had been so broken when he met her it was obvious that she'd never really recovered from the loss of her parents. And she didn't have any siblings to lean on. He couldn't imagine what her life must have been like after such a tragedy. The large, empty castle must have felt like a tomb.

When the Duke of Weselton had visited the Southern Isles the previous fall, he had spoken at length about Arendelle and its orphaned princess and who would take over her kingdom. His twelve older brothers hadn't paid any attention, but Hans had listened closely. Why should they bother? Most of them already knew their place in their kingdom; some of them had a chance to rule the islands or had married well and would rule elsewhere. As thirteenth in line, his chances of ruling were slim. He was the only one who knew what it was like to have to find a place to fit in the world. He could understand Elsa in a way no one else could. He had decided right then that he would journey to meet her. The Duke of Weselton, a devious fellow who was always looking for a new partnership, had been delighted. Hans had been residing in Arendelle ever since.

Yes, there were parts of home he missed. His brothers (sometimes), his father's wisdom (all the time), and his islands, which were warmer and lusher than Arendelle. The problem was the Southern Isles never really seemed like they were going to be his kingdom.

Arendelle, on the other hand, just might be.

Hans stared out one of the windows into the courtyard and watched the castle workers hurrying around, hanging banners and decorations for Elsa's coronation. After three long years, the kingdom was ready to have a queen.

What they needed even more was a *king*. He and Elsa weren't officially courting—he didn't want to scare her off with such a declaration—but it seemed like they were pretty close.

"I'm ready," Elsa said. He heard a crash come from her room behind them. The princess winced. "Something must have fallen. I'm sure it's nothing to worry about!"

Elsa kept many secrets. He had to admire her for that. "Shall we walk?"

She nodded. "Yes. I think you were right. Air will do me good."

"It will," he agreed. The two stared at each other for a moment.

Hans hoped she liked what she saw. He had reddish-brown hair and muttonchops, which none of his brothers shared and which they constantly teased him about. His mother said they suited him. His brothers all had brown eyes, while his were hazel, like his mother's. He was taller than the princess by several inches, and very lanky, which came from running away from twelve older brothers. Elsa reminded him of a deer—timid and easily frightened, with large blue eyes that held pools of sadness.

"So I was thinking—let's forget the courtyard. It's

packed with people." Hans led her down the long hall. "Let's go somewhere quieter. How about the stables? It's been a while since I've been down there to see Sitron."

"The stables," Elsa said slowly. She definitely seemed to like Hans's horse, Sitron. He was so docile. "I think that's a great idea."

She paused in front of the large portrait of her family that hung in the hall. Her parents looked down on her from the wall. In the painting, they each had one hand on their young daughter's shoulders. She looked like she was around eight.

"I used to fantasize about being an only child," Hans admitted. "What was it really like? Who did you play with on a rainy day? Or cheat from on your schoolwork? Or go sledding with when it snowed?"

Elsa thought for a moment. "I was quiet and always handed in my schoolwork early—and did it on my own."

He smirked. "Show-off. My brothers were always getting me in trouble with our governess, sending papers flying into the back of her head and blaming it on me. Have I told you how three of them pretended I was invisible? Literally! For two years!"

Elsa's eyes widened. "That's horrible!"

Hans shrugged. "That's what brothers do."

"I wouldn't know," Elsa said, and looked away.

He didn't skip a beat. "But you must have had friends."

"My parents let me play with the staff's children, and sometimes they'd invite dukes or nobles to come for a party and I'd play with their kids," she explained, "but there was no one I was really close with." She looked at him sidelong. "I have a feeling my childhood was a lot lonelier than yours."

"That very well may be, but at least you weren't always competing for attention and trying to figure out where you belonged." Hans paused. "Your childhood may have been lonely, but your future won't be. I'm sure you'll have a family of your own someday." She blushed and looked away again, but he kept going. "And you'll probably want more than one heir for the kingdom. I'm surprised your parents didn't."

"My mother couldn't have any more children after me," Elsa said softly. "But I've often wondered . . . No, it's ridiculous."

"What?" he asked earnestly. It wasn't often she opened up, but when she did, he glimpsed the princess she might have been before the tragedy.

Elsa looked around sheepishly. "It's silly."

"I like silly," he said, and spun her around.

She laughed and studied his face for a moment before speaking. "I always wanted a sister," she blurted out. "I feel bad saying that, but sometimes I'd fantasize about having a little sister." She blushed. "I told you it was silly."

"Not silly," he said. "It sounds like you were lonely." He held her hand, and she looked at him in surprise. "But you don't have to be anymore."

Elsa squeezed his hand. "I like talking to you."

"I'm glad." Finally, he was making progress! "I've been searching so long for a place of my own, but with you, I think I may have found it." Elsa opened her mouth to say something.

Down the hall, a door slammed, and Lord Peterssen emerged with the Duke of Weselton. Neither saw them.

"Maybe we should call the princess down to go over her coronation speech one more time," they heard the Duke say. "It needs to be just right."

Elsa tried to back away. He held tight and pulled her through an open door and out of sight. The two of them broke into a run, laughing as they raced through the portrait hall and other rooms, till they made their way outside into the sun and to freedom.

When they finally reached the stables, Elsa stopped to catch her breath. "I can't remember the last time I ran off like that!" she said, laughing.

"Sometimes you need an escape," Hans said. It was what he had done. He didn't add that part.

Elsa spread her arms wide and spun around. "It's liberating!"

He'd never seen her act that free. He had her exactly where he wanted her.

He walked to the stables and opened some of the upper doors to the barn. Horses immediately poked their heads out. Sitron appeared, his white-and-black mane blowing softly in the wind. Hans petted his mane while Elsa stepped over to rub his dun coat. The two of them concentrated on the horse instead of each other. The stables were completely quiet.

"You know, it's crazy," Hans said, "but I've never met someone who thinks so much . . ."

"Like you?" Elsa said, looking as surprised as he was.

"Yes." Hans searched her face. "Maybe you and I were just meant . . ."

"To be," Elsa said, finishing his sentence for him again.

They both started to laugh. Maybe an official courting was even closer than he thought.

"The Duke would be thrilled," Elsa said wryly.

She had the man pegged. "So would Lord Peterssen," Hans said, brushing Sitron's side with his hand. "I've heard them talking. They think we're a strong match." *To lead this kingdom.* He snuck a glance at her.

Elsa's face was hard to read. "Do they?"

You know they do, he wanted to say, but he stayed patient. He'd gotten that far. He was much closer than he had been even a week before. "But it doesn't matter what they think. It matters what we think." He glanced her way again.

"Exactly. I like how we are right now at this very moment."

Hans tried not to look disappointed. "Me too."

The Duke wanted a proposal to come before the coronation, but Hans knew that might be tricky. An engagement didn't have to come that day. Or the next. Hans knew in his heart that they were going to rule Arendelle together soon enough.

If Elsa was smart, she'd let him take the lead. And if she didn't . . . well, accidents happened. All Arendelle would need to survive was their new king.

CHAPTER ELEVEN

Anna

This was it! It was finally the day!

Anna stared at the big red circle she'd placed on the calendar and tried not to scream with excitement. She grabbed a pillow from her bed and squealed into it quietly instead. She'd been waiting for this day for three years!

Three years of planning, counting down, and dreaming.

Three years to figure out exactly what she was going to say to her parents.

And in three years, she still hadn't figured out the right words to tell them her plan.

Ma, Papa, I'm eighteen now, Anna rehearsed for the billionth time in her head. *I'm all grown up, and it's time I started my life, which is why I'm . . . I'm . . .*

This was always the part that gave her pause.

Every time she thought about telling her parents she was leaving Harmon, she got a massive stomachache. These were her parents. They'd taken her in as a baby, loved her, and cared for her. She didn't want to hurt them.

I wish Freya were here.

That thought popped into her head a lot. Even though it had been three years since Freya had been lost at sea with the king and queen, Anna still thought about her every day. If anyone could have convinced Anna's mother that Arendelle was a wonderful place to start a life, it was her. And Anna's mother would have been relieved to know Anna had people like family watching over her nearby.

But Freya was gone. Anna had to do this on her own.

The pink room she had adored for so long felt like a child's now, but she still loved every inch of the space, especially her window seat, with its view of life at the bottom of the mountain. Arendelle seemed so close and yet so far away. Anna touched one of the wooden castle spires on the model her father had made her long before. Tears sprang to her eyes. Her parents loved her so much. How would she tell them without breaking their hearts?

With food!

Of course!

She'd bake them the most perfect dessert she could.

Something they didn't make in the bakery every day. They'd be so happy with her creation, and their stomachs so satisfied, that they'd have to hear her out about Arendelle. And she knew just the thing to bake: carrot cake!

She'd made carrot cake for Papa once before, and he had loved it so much he had eaten it every day for a week. Ma had complained he was having too much sugar, and he had said, "I own a bakery! Of course I eat too much sugar!" And they all laughed and agreed that carrot cake was the best thing Anna had ever made.

That was the cake she needed to make them agree to her plan.

She looked at the clock. After baking all morning, her parents were likely on their break, relaxing in the parlor. Papa might even be taking a nap. She'd slip out unnoticed and return fast to get to work. The cake would be ready in time for supper. They could even have cake *for* supper! She'd always wanted to try that.

Anna headed out the door, the heat of summer blasting her in the face. *What ingredients do I need? I have everything but carrots, right? We own a bakery,* she reminded herself, not watching where she was going. *What else could I possibly—WHOA!*

She ran smack into a young man holding a giant block of ice. The impact sent the ice flying. The block smashed to the ground, breaking into a million pieces in front of the market.

"Hey!" the stranger barked. "You're going to need to pay for—" He spun around and looked at her in surprise. "Oh." His eyes widened, and he stepped back. "It's you."

"You mean it's *you!*" Anna was equally surprised. She remembered him from years before. She had looked for him several times but had never seen him again. "You're the boy who talks to his reindeer."

As if on cue, the reindeer walked into view, nudging the stranger in the back.

"Not a boy, first of all. And I talk *for* my reindeer," he said. "His name is Sven. He wanted carrots, but now that you broke my ice delivery, he won't get any."

The reindeer snorted.

He turned to the animal. "I'm not being rude," he whispered gruffly. "She broke the ice. Now we don't get carrots." The reindeer snorted louder. "Fine!" He spun around again. "Sven said I'm barking at you." Kristoff looked at his feet. "So sorry . . . even though it was your fault."

"It was an accident," Anna said. She couldn't help noticing the way his shaggy blond hair fell in front of his brown eyes. The two of them stared at each other for a moment. Then they both looked away. "I'll pay you in cookies if you want," she offered. "I make the best ones in the village."

The reindeer started to prance.

"You make the *only* ones in the village," the young man deadpanned.

"How would you know?" Anna replied. "Did you ask about me?"

He pulled his wool cap down on his head. "No. Maybe."

She flushed. "I'm Anna. My parents own Tomally's Baked Goods. What's your name?"

"Kristoff," he said, then turned to his reindeer. "Sven, we need to go get more ice before—"

At that moment, Goran emerged from the market, saw the ice on the ground, and placed his hands on his head. "No! I've been waiting for this delivery all morning!"

Anna winced. Goran had run the market as long as she could remember. Her parents had always been thankful that he was agreeable to bartering goods. A well-timed cinnamon roll had won her favor sometimes when she forgot money for groceries.

"I'm sorry. It was out of my control." Kristoff side-eyed Anna. "I can get you more, but it will take a few hours."

"A few hours? I needed this ice *now* to keep my groceries cool in this heat!" Goran complained.

"I can get it to you this afternoon," Kristoff promised,

"but if I could get the supplies I need now, I can get it faster. My ice ax is pretty dull. And Sven is out of carrots." The reindeer snorted.

Goran folded his arms across his chest. "No ice, no trade."

"But you've done it before," Kristoff reminded him, getting annoyed. "Help me out!"

"Not today!" Goran folded his arms across his chest. "I needed that ice now."

"Goran, maybe I can help. How about some cinnamon—" Anna started, but Kristoff stared her down.

"Back up while I deal with this crook here."

Goran narrowed his eyes and stood up straighter. Anna had never noticed how tall he was. He was bigger than Kristoff. "What did you call me?"

Kristoff stood nose to nose with him. "I said—"

Anna jumped between them. "Okay, I think this is my fault! You need ice, he needs an ice ax to get the ice. Can't we come to some sort of arrangement?"

"I don't need your help," Kristoff said.

"Actually, you do," Goran growled.

"Goran, put the carrots and ice ax on my tab," Anna insisted. "I'll be back with some cinnamon rolls to keep you happy, and then Kristoff will return with ice before you know it." Anna looked from one man to the other. "All right with everyone?"

Goran silently handed Anna the carrots, then went inside the market to retrieve the ice ax. Anna smiled at Kristoff, feeling pleased, but he didn't share her joy.

"I don't do handouts," he said.

"Who said it's a handout? You'll pay Goran back, and if you want to pay me in ice, too, now you know where to find me." She divided the bunch of carrots in half, handed Kristoff some, and patted the reindeer on the head. "Bye, Sven!"

Anna practically skipped down the street back home. She had a feeling she'd see Kristoff again.

But first she needed to bake. The quicker it was finished, the quicker she could finally get this conversation over with. She was ticking off bakery measurements in her head when her parents walked into the room talking.

"Nothing has changed, Johan. It's been three years! Maybe nothing ever will. She has the right to know the truth," Ma was saying.

"Who has the right to know the truth?" Anna asked as she gathered several bowls and large spoons. "And you're supposed to be resting! Now you've ruined my surprise!" Anna was trying to be funny, but her parents looked uneasy. "What's going on? Is this about me?"

Papa and Ma glanced at each other.

Papa looked uncomfortable. "We don't really know how

to tell you this, Anna Bear, without possibly betraying our closest friend."

Closest friend? Betrayal? "Is this about Freya?" Anna asked.

Ma nodded. "She's my oldest and dearest friend—she always will be."

"Of course she is," Anna said. Her mother had never really gotten over Freya's death, and neither had she. "I think about her all the time, too."

"You do?" Papa asked.

"Of course. It's kind of why I wanted to make you this carrot cake today. I have something to tell you, as well, but now that you're talking about betrayal I'm getting worried."

Ma reached for her arm. "We don't mean to alarm you. Your papa and I have just been discussing something—"

"For the past three years," Papa said under his breath.

"And we don't want to keep you in the dark anymore," Ma added. "But the situation is complicated."

"We made a promise to Freya," Papa said. "But we also don't want you spending your whole life not knowing the truth."

Anna's eyes widened. "So this *is* about me . . . and Freya?"

Papa sounded like he was having trouble breathing. "Yes and no."

They were truly scaring her. "What is going on?"

"I knew her a lot longer than you did, Johan," Ma told him. "If this curse never lifts, she—"

"Curse?" Anna's arm slipped and she knocked a bowl off the table. It shattered. Papa grabbed the broom from the hook on the wall and began sweeping it up. "I'm sorry! I thought there was no such thing as curses . . . is there?"

Ma hesitated and looked at Papa. "I don't mean curse, exactly. It's just a word."

"A word for something made up," Anna clarified.

Ma didn't answer her. "Johan, if things don't change, she will live her whole life not knowing she has another family out there."

Papa stopped sweeping. *"We're* her family, Tomally," he said softly. "What good would telling her do? She can't change things. Who would even believe her?"

Ma's eyes filled with tears. "You're right. I don't want to put our daughter in harm's way, but I also don't want to carry this secret to my grave."

Their conversation wasn't making sense to her. "Is this about my birth parents?"

The frown lines on her mother's forehead deepened. "Well, yes . . ."

"Did Freya know them?" Anna asked. She'd always wondered. Freya had been such a big part of her life since the beginning. Maybe Freya had known something Anna didn't. Silence hung over the room as they stared at one another. "It's okay," Anna finally said. "If you know who they are and don't want to tell me, I'll understand. It doesn't matter anyway." She reached for their hands. "You've been the best parents anyone could ever hope for."

Papa and Ma reached in for a hug at the same time. They were a family of huggers and laughers. Anna clung to them, not wanting to let go.

Papa looked at her with tears in his eyes as well. "Anna Bear, these aren't our secrets to tell. We hope you can respect that."

"I can, but I do have a secret of my own that I wanted to share with you." Her cake wasn't ready, but since they were sharing, it was the perfect time to tell them. "And it has to do with Freya, too."

Ma looked rattled. "It isn't . . . Do you know . . ."

Anna could feel her heart thumping. Her lips were suddenly dry, but she couldn't stop now. She thought of how Freya had always said *Be true to yourself.* This was her being true. "I want to move to Arendelle."

Her parents stood perfectly still. Anna kept going.

"You both know I've wanted to live in Arendelle for as long as I can remember. I love Harmon, but it feels like there is a whole big world out there that I'm missing out on. A world at the bottom of this mountain." Anna pointed to the window where Arendelle was visible. "I promise I'm not moving there without a plan. I'm going to open my own bakery when I make enough money, and until I do, I'll work in a bakery near the castle. Freya always said there were several. Several! Not just one, like we have here."

Her parents still appeared tongue-tied.

"I know I'll be far away, but I'll visit, and you can visit, too." They hadn't interrupted her yet, so she kept going. "I'm eighteen and it's time I started my own life. Freya always talked about how much I'd like Arendelle, and I know she was right."

Her mother nodded knowingly, filling Anna with hope.

"I think you are too young," Papa blurted out.

"I'm eighteen," Anna whispered.

"Johan," her mother started.

He shook his head. "Tomally, you know I'm right. A woman is of age at twenty-one. I'm sorry, Anna, but you are not ready. It isn't . . . safe." He looked at Ma. "Arendelle isn't the right place for you right now. We need you here."

"Ma?" Anna said, but Ma shook her head.

"Papa is right," Ma said. "We are getting older, Anna Bear, and this bakery is a lot for us to handle. It was always our dream that someday you would run it."

The idea touched Anna greatly. She knew her parents

were tired of being up before dawn and baking all day. But staying in Harmon forever wasn't what she wanted. She could feel it in her bones and see it in her dreams—dreams full of snow and voices. Sometimes it felt as if someone was looking for her. But that was silly.

"You know I love this shop, and I love being with you, but I've always dreamt of living in Arendelle," Anna told them gently. "I feel like I'm meant for something bigger. Life is short. Losing Freya taught me that. I don't want to wait another day to start my life."

Ma and Papa kept looking at each other.

"She isn't ready," Papa said firmly to Ma. "It isn't safe. . . ."

"I know." Ma looked at Anna. "We want you to have the life you dream of—a life in Arendelle—and you will have it. I know it in my heart just as you do, Anna Bear." She squeezed her hand. "It just isn't your time yet. Trust us."

"I understand," Anna said, but she truly didn't. She blinked back tears and held her tongue. She never disobeyed her parents, and she wasn't about to now, but three years felt like a long time to wait.

CHAPTER TWELVE

Elsa

I wish I had the power to stop time, Elsa thought as she stood at her bedroom window, watching people flood into the castle courtyard toward her family's bronze statue. The gates were open and the chapel was prepped. The choir she'd heard practicing for days was ready to perform. But the time for her own rehearsals was over. She should stop worrying, but she knew she couldn't. Time seemed like it was roaring ahead, and Elsa couldn't slow it down.

She had already gotten dressed with Gerda's help. Her gown was beautiful, but it wasn't designed for comfort. And it wasn't created with her in mind. It almost felt as if she were a doll playing dress up, living in someone else's body. But she kept reminding herself the dress only had to be worn for a few hours. She could manage until then. There was nothing left to do but wait to be called.

I wish I could stop time, Elsa wished again, but she knew it wasn't possible.

Being with Hans the other day had put her mind at ease, but standing in her room again, she couldn't escape her thoughts. *Papa and Mama, I wish you were standing here beside me. I can't do this alone.*

Elsa heard grunting and turned around. Olaf was trying to move her hope chest and failing.

"Olaf!" Elsa hurried over. "What are you doing?"

"Looking for Anna," he explained. "She should be here for this."

Elsa leaned down, her sadness almost overwhelming her. "We don't even know who Anna is."

"I know she'd want to see you, though!" the snowman said brightly. "Maybe she's in this hope chest. She loved to hide in here."

Elsa was about to ask Olaf what he meant when she heard the knock at her door.

The time had come.

Olaf reached out to hug her. "Good luck!" He ran to hide behind her bed. "I'll be waiting when you get back."

Elsa opened the door. Hans was waiting in a white

dress uniform. "Princess," he said with a smile, and held out his arm, "are you ready to be escorted to the chapel?"

No, she wanted to say, but she was happy to see him standing there. Hans was so thoughtful. He had offered to escort her to the ceremony, and she had agreed, knowing his presence was calming.

"Ah, look at this!" said the Duke, appearing out of nowhere. "The very picture of young love."

The Duke, on the other hand, was not calming. What was he doing there?

He adjusted his wire-rimmed glasses and looked up at them over the edge of his ample nose. He had slicked his white hair back for the occasion and was in full military dress, with a gold sash and medals swinging from his jacket. "What a fine day this will be for the two of you!"

Lord Peterssen rushed down the hall toward them. "I believe the *future queen* decided Prince Hans would be escorting her to the ceremony." Then he motioned to the Duke. "Why don't I take you down and help you find a seat near the front?"

Thank goodness for Lord Peterssen!

The Duke ignored him. "I was just thinking about how elated the people will be to see Hans of the Southern Isles on her arm publicly for the first time. They're not only getting a queen, they're getting a potential king, too. Today would be a fine day to announce their union. Don't you think?"

Elsa blushed. Lord Peterssen shifted uncomfortably. Hans looked away.

She was growing tired of the Duke's pushiness. Marriage was not on her mind. She and Hans had developed a lovely friendship that could perhaps become more, but she had a crown to think of first and secrets that were consuming her. Plus, it was her coronation day.

Elsa heard a crash inside her room. *Olaf!*

"Your Grace, Elsa and I have already discussed this." Hans's voice was curt. "Her duties come first." Lord Peterssen nodded agreeably.

"Of course, but still, announcing an engagement today, when Elsa is standing in front of her kingdom, would show them she will be a queen of the people," the Duke insisted.

She couldn't believe what she was hearing. Anger bubbled up inside her.

"Princess?" the Duke pressed. "Don't you agree?"

"I think this conversation should take place later," Lord Peterssen said, checking his pocket watch. "The chapel is already full. We should be starting the ceremony soon."

Hans looked at Elsa questioningly. "He brings up a good point, but the decision rests with you. What do you think?"

"I . . ." Elsa hesitated, feeling her fingers starting to tingle. No matter how much she enjoyed Hans's company, they'd only known each other a short while. She couldn't put her finger on it, but something was definitely holding her back.

"Have you even properly asked the princess?" the Duke asked, hitting Hans in the arm. "A princess deserves a proper proposal."

Hans's cheeks turned red. "No, but—"

"Ask the girl!" the Duke said jovially. Lord Peterssen ran a hand through his thinning hair. "Today is the day!"

"Elsa!" It was Olaf. He had never yelled to her when she was with people. "Elsa!" Maybe he was in trouble!

Lord Peterssen looked puzzled.

"Forgive me, but I think I left something in my room," she said. Her whole body was starting to tingle.

Hans didn't seem to hear her, because he was already getting down on one knee.

The sensation had never taken over her whole body before. Suddenly, she felt as if the walls were closing in. She had to get to Olaf.

The prince looked up at her shyly. "Princess Elsa of Arendelle, will you marry me?"

"*Elsa!*" Olaf called again, louder than before.

"I believe Gerda is calling me," Elsa said sheepishly,

and looked down at Hans. Her face felt flushed. "Would you excuse me for a moment?"

Hans couldn't hide his surprise. "Yes, by all means . . ." He trailed off.

The Duke sighed. "We will wait for you—and your answer," he said with a thin smile.

Hans stood up quickly and adjusted the medals on his jacket. He didn't make eye contact with her. The whole situation was uncomfortable, and the Duke was making it worse. She was upset, but she had to get to Olaf and see what was wrong.

Elsa opened the door a crack, slipped inside, and shut the door. Olaf was standing right behind her, hopping up and down.

"Olaf, what is the matter?" Elsa whispered. "You can't shout like that. Someone—"

"I think I found something!" he cheered. "I pushed your hope chest too far and it banged into the desk and your lockbox fell off. Come see!"

Her green lockbox was on its side, empty. The interior of the lid should have had a lining draping across, but now it was sagging and showed a hollow section in the top arch. It looked like something was behind it.

"See?" Olaf pointed to the liner. "My hands can't fit

just right to pull it away, but something is behind that green stuff. Look! Look!"

Olaf wasn't wrong. Gently, she pulled the velvet away, revealing the hollowed-out top. A canvas had been carefully hidden inside.

Elsa quickly unfolded it. She was astonished to see it was a painting.

At first glance, it looked like the portrait of her family that hung in the Great Hall. But this painting had four people in it: the king, the queen, Elsa, and another little girl.

The child was a few years younger than Elsa, and she was the spitting image of the king. She had wide-set blue eyes, bright red hair set in pigtails, and a sprinkle of freckles dotting her nose. She wore a pale green dress, and she was clutching Elsa's arm as if she might never let go.

Elsa touched the painting and started to cry. "It's Anna!" she said. She knew it for certain.

The memories flooded her body so quickly she felt like she was drowning.

"I remember," Elsa said in surprise, and then she collapsed on the floor.

CHAPTER THIRTEEN

Elsa

Thirteen Years Earlier . . .

The flour was everywhere.

It blanketed the floor, was sprinkled all over the wood table, and had made its way into Anna's hair. The five-year-old didn't mind. She lifted another scoop of flour from the jar and threw it into the air.

"It looks like snow!" Anna said as the flour rained down. One of her pigtails was falling out, even though her hair had just been done an hour earlier. "Try it, Elsa! Try it!"

"You're making a mess." Elsa smiled despite herself and tried to tidy up behind her.

"Princess Anna, *please* try to keep the flour in the bowl," Olina begged.

"But it's so much fun to throw, Miss Olina!" Anna said, giggling as she tossed more flour into the air.

"Why don't you two prepare the dough and I'll get the stove ready?" Olina suggested.

"Okay, Anna, you can come help me." Elsa pushed a loose strand of blond hair off her face and creamed the soft butter by hand with a wooden spoon. Anna climbed up on a stool next to Elsa and watched.

Together, they added the sugar, flour, vanilla extract, and milk. They took turns stirring until the cookie mixture was a smooth pale yellow. Elsa cracked the eggs, since the last time Anna did them, she'd gotten shells in a batch of cookies they served to the king of Sondringham.

Elsa was still stirring the mixture when Anna got bored and started racing around the kitchen. Elsa laughed, abandoning her spoon and running after her. Suddenly, Mama swooped in and grabbed both of them.

"This looks wonderful, girls," Mama said. "Your father is going to be so surprised. You know how much he loves your krumkaker."

"Crumbs cake-r." Anna tried hard to say the word, but she never could. "Crumb cake?"

Mama and Elsa laughed.

"Krumkaker," Mama said, the word rolling off her tongue smoothly. "I've been using this recipe since I was your age. I used to bake these with my best friend."

"That's where you learned to bake with love," Anna said.

"Yes, I did," Mama agreed, fixing Anna's right pigtail.

Together, they huddled around the stove as Olina lit it and placed the decorative two-sided iron griddle on top of the flame to heat up. Their krumkake griddle had the Arendelle coat of arms on it, a touch their father loved. Mama poured the first scoop of batter into the center of the griddle and closed it, holding it over the flame. Together, they counted to ten; then she flipped the griddle over and they counted out ten seconds again. The hardest part of the process was removing the baked dough from the griddle so they could mold it around a cone-shaped rolling pin to form the cookie. Olina and Mama never let them help with that part. Olina claimed she had calluses on her fingertips from getting burned by the griddle one too many times. But when the cookie was cool, it was removed from the cone, and that was when both girls were allowed to sprinkle it with powdered sugar. Sometimes they left the cookies hollow, and other times they filled them with a sweet, creamy filling. Papa liked them plain. Before they knew it, they'd made half a dozen cookies and had enough batter to make at least a dozen more.

"Why don't you three keep going and I'll be right back?" Olina told them, wiping her hands on her apron. "I just need to accept this vegetable delivery."

"Can I try using the griddle? Please? Can I try?" Anna begged.

"No, darling," Mama told her. "You'll burn your fingers." Anna watched her mother remove the griddle from the stove and pull the baked dough out of it. She wrapped it around the krumkake pin to form its shape.

"Your Majesty?" Kai appeared in the kitchen doorway. "The king has asked for you to make an appearance in the council chambers."

Mama looked at the girls. "I'll be right back," she promised. "Don't touch the griddle till Olina or I return."

Elsa nodded, but by the time she turned around, Anna was already on her tippy-toes, scooping the batter onto the middle of the griddle. "Anna! Mama said not to touch it."

"I can do it," Anna insisted, counting to herself and flipping the griddle. "I want to bake my own cookie for Papa."

"Wait for Miss Olina," Elsa told her, but Anna was impulsive. She hated rules.

Elsa, on the other hand, swore by them.

Anna opened the griddle and tried to pull the crispy dough from the middle of the grate. "Ouch!" she cried, dropping the dough onto the floor and waving her fingers frantically. "I got burned!" Anna burst into tears.

"Let me see." Elsa grabbed her sister's hand. Two of her fingers were bright red. Elsa needed something cold to put on Anna's hand to stop the burning sensation. She spotted a copper pot full of water on the table. Olina wouldn't be back for a few minutes. Elsa hovered her fingertips over the pot and concentrated on the water. Seconds later, a blue glow appeared around her hands, and snowflakes and crystals began to flow.

Anna stopped crying. "Oooh."

Within seconds, the water in the pot was frozen solid.

"Put your hand on here to cool it down," Elsa instructed as the ice crackled. Anna ran over to touch it. Neither of them heard their mother return.

"Girls!" Mama's voice was dangerously low.

Elsa hid her hands behind her back, but it was too late. She had disobeyed Mama by using her gift in public, where someone else might see.

"You know better than to—"

"How are the cookies coming?" Olina asked, returning with a basket of fresh vegetables, which she placed on the counter. She started when she noticed the copper pot she had just filled with water. "My word! What happened to my pot? How could the water freeze on such a warm night?"

Mama pulled Anna and Elsa to her sides. "Strange, indeed! Olina, Anna burned her fingers on the stove. I'm going to bandage them and get the girls to bed."

"But the cookies . . ." Elsa protested.

Her mother flashed her a sharp look. "Olina will finish

them and you can give the cookies to your father over breakfast. We're done baking this evening."

Olina didn't say anything. She was still too busy staring at the pot in wonder.

Elsa hung her head. "Yes, Mama."

In the girls' shared bedroom, Mama applied a salve to Anna's fingers and dressed her in her favorite green nightgown, then sent Anna to fetch Papa for story time. Moonlight streaked through the large triangular window as Elsa changed into her blue nightgown behind the dressing panel. She could hear their mother singing a lullaby as she picked up a few dolls Anna had left on the floor. By the time Elsa climbed into her bed, Mama was by her side.

"I'm so sorry, Mama," Elsa said, still feeling bad.

Her mother sat on the edge of her bed. "I know. And I know it's not your fault that Anna got hurt. Olina or I should have been watching, but when we can't . . ."

"It's my duty to watch over Anna," Elsa recited diligently.

"No," Mama said. "It's your job to be a good big sister, but also to protect yourself. What if Olina had walked in when you were using your gift?"

Elsa noticed the worry lines on her mother's forehead. She hated upsetting her. "She didn't see me."

"But she could have," Mama reminded her. "You must be more careful, Elsa. Papa and I know your gift is truly special, but until we know more about it, we want it to be our family secret. Do you understand?" Elsa nodded. "Your father has been trying to learn everything he can. He spends hours in the library reading." She looked down at their hands and took Elsa's in hers. "So far, we have found nothing that explains how you could have been born with such powers."

Powers. It was a word her mother had never used before to explain her gift. It did feel powerful, seeing the ice shoot out with just the slightest thought. Sometimes she didn't have to think about the ice, and it just happened on its own.

Mama held her hand tighter. "For now, we need you to promise to only use your gift when you are around your father, Anna, and me."

Elsa looked down. "Yes, Mama, but . . . sometimes I don't know how to control the ice," she admitted. "When I get upset, it's even worse. I know Papa says to conceal, don't feel. But sometimes when I feel too much, I don't know how to manage the snow."

Her mother hugged her. "We will learn to control your gift so that it doesn't control you. I promise!"

"Really?" Elsa looked hopeful.

"Yes, all we want is to keep you safe," Mama said. "Both of you."

Just then, they heard Anna's giggles coming down the hallway, followed by a big belly laugh from Papa.

"I will be more careful," Elsa whispered.

"Good girl." Mama kissed her cheek.

They looked at the door as Anna and Papa burst into the room, Anna hanging upside down as Papa hung on to her ankles. "Who's ready for a bedtime story?" Papa asked.

"Elsa? Psst . . . Elsa? Wake up, wake up, wake up!"

Elsa's eyes remained closed. "Anna, go back to sleep."

She felt Anna climb onto her bed and dramatically collapse on top of her. "I just can't. The sky's awake! So I'm awake! So we have to play!"

Elsa opened one eye and pushed Anna off her. "Go play by yourself!"

She heard Anna's body hit the floor and waited for the cry that would tell her whether Anna had hurt herself. That made her feel slightly guilty—until she felt Anna pulling open one of her eyelids.

"Do you want to build a snowman?" Anna asked coyly.

Elsa couldn't help sitting up and smiling.

It was the middle of the night.

That meant the castle and all its occupants were fast asleep.

She wouldn't be seen. No one would be frightened.

If there was ever a time for Elsa to practice her gift, that was it.

Seconds later, they were out of their room, with Anna in boots and Elsa in her slippers, and they rushed down the stairs. Elsa kept shushing Anna while Anna kept whispering, "Come on! Come on! Come on!"

They hurried into the deserted Great Hall. The room was massive, with large vaulted ceilings and ornate wooden details and wallpaper. Usually it was decorated for parties, but that night it was empty. They skidded to a stop in the center of the room.

"Do the magic! Do the magic!" Anna jumped up and down with excitement.

Elsa glanced at the doors to make sure they were closed. Satisfied, she started to roll her hands round and round. A snowball formed between her palms, surrounded by a blue glow. "Ready?" she asked, feeling the rush she got when she was about to use magic. She threw her hands up and flung the snowball high into the air. Snow started to fall from the ceiling, washing the floor in a blanket of white.

"This is amazing!" Anna marveled, her giggles of joy filling Elsa with pride. Anna, more than anyone else, loved Elsa's gift, and she begged her to use it often. Their parents, on the other hand, wanted her to keep it private. But if a gift like this could bring such joy, shouldn't she share it? Besides, she loved impressing her sister.

"Watch this," Elsa said, and stomped her foot. Ice began to crackle and cover the floor, like it was their own personal ice-skating rink. Seeing Anna's delight only made Elsa want to create more. She concentrated harder and snow kept falling, ice kept crackling, and the room soon became a winter wonderland. Next it was time to make the snowman Anna loved so much. They rolled his round bottom, then stacked two more snowballs on top. Elsa's was perfectly round, but the head Anna made was more of a cylinder. Anna dashed to the kitchen downstairs to grab a carrot for the snowman's nose and snag some coal for his eyes and belly. They snatched some twigs from the fireplace to create his arms and hair.

Finished, Elsa stood behind the snowman as Anna watched from one of their parents' thrones, and Elsa pretended he was alive. "Hi, I'm Olaf," she said in a funny voice, "and I like warm hugs."

Anna jumped out of the throne and threw herself at the snowman, almost knocking off his head. "I love you, Olaf!"

Anna wouldn't let Olaf out of her sight, so Elsa pushed him around the room as Anna hung on, using him as her skating partner. Next Anna wanted to jump snow mounds. Elsa complied, making more and more snow so Anna could leap from one pile to the next.

"Hang on!" Elsa told her.

"Catch me!" Anna squealed with delight as she pounced from pile to pile in her green nightgown, jumping faster and faster. Elsa struggled to make snow quicker than Anna could jump. "Again!" Anna shouted.

"Wait!" Elsa created the snow piles faster, but she was only one ahead of Anna now. "Slow down!" she cried, but Anna didn't listen. Elsa backed up to give herself more room and felt herself slip and fall. By the time she looked up, Anna was already in midair with nothing beneath her feet. "Anna!" Elsa panicked, shooting the snow into the air as fast as possible.

The stream of magic collided with Anna, hitting her in the face.

Anna tumbled down the nearest snow pile. She wasn't moving.

Elsa rushed to her side. "Anna!" she cried, taking her little sister into her arms, but Anna wouldn't wake up. A streak of white hair slowly wove itself through her red locks.

Fear bubbled up inside Elsa, her breath caught in her throat, and her whole body began to tremble. "Mama! Papa!" she cried at the top of her lungs. The ice around the sisters began to crack and grow, covering the entire floor and crawling up the walls. It thickened and rumbled, knocking over Olaf, who broke into pieces. "You're okay, Anna," Elsa cried, cradling her in her arms. "I've got you."

When their parents ran into the room, they saw Elsa sitting with Anna's motionless body. Mama looked so frightened Elsa's terror grew, causing the ice to spread further.

"Elsa, what have you done?" Papa shouted. "This is getting out of hand."

"It was an accident. I'm sorry, Anna," Elsa said, her voice trembling as Mama took Anna from her.

"She's ice cold," Mama said quietly, fear seeping into her voice.

"I know where we have to go," Papa said, moving quickly and motioning for Elsa and Mama to follow.

"Is Anna going to be okay? Mama? Will she be okay?" Elsa whispered. She had never been more frightened. But no one answered her. Elsa choked back sobs.

This was why her parents told her to be careful when using her gift. Look what had happened to Anna. If that was what her powers could do, she didn't want them anymore.

Why did her magic have to ruin everything? Why couldn't she be normal like everyone else? Anger pulsed inside her, and she felt her heart beat faster. Snow started to swirl around her fingertips, and she couldn't stop it.

No! She took a few deep breaths, trying to calm down.

"Elsa!" her mother called.

Elsa followed her mother into the library and watched

her lock the door behind her. Mama wrapped Anna in a blue blanket and held her tight while Papa pulled books off the shelf, searching for something. No one spoke. If anything happened to her sister, Elsa would never forgive herself.

"This is it," Papa said, holding up a red book. It looked rather old, and Elsa didn't understand the writing when he opened it in front of them. The book was full of symbols. There was a picture of a troll standing over a body with a blue spirit seeping out of the person's head.

"Yes, this is the one," Mama agreed as a map fell out of the book and fluttered to the floor.

Elsa noticed the map was of Arendelle, with markings that pointed to a place in the mountains.

Papa touched Anna's forehead. "She's still so cold."

"We have to go to them," Mama said. "We can't wait."

"We can take the horses," Papa said. "Elsa, come with us. Quietly, now."

"Mama, will Anna be okay?" Elsa asked again.

"Hush now," Mama said, and Elsa did as she was told. "We have to get to the stables unseen."

The castle was eerily silent, as if every part of it were shunning Elsa for her mistake. Elsa didn't ask questions. She followed her parents into the stables and watched Papa saddle up their horses. He helped Mama onto one and placed Anna in her arms. Then he motioned for Elsa, and he picked her up and placed her in front of him on his horse. Seconds later, Papa raced out of the stables. Mama was right beside him. The two horses gained speed as they ran out the castle gates and into the night.

Elsa concentrated on the path in front of her and tried to remain calm, but she kept freezing things around her without even realizing it. Papa clutched the map from the book and used the northern lights as his guide. Higher and higher into the mountains they climbed, the sea seeming to shrink away. At one point, she could have sworn she heard a boy's voice, but when she turned around, all she saw was a baby reindeer. Seconds later, it was gone.

"We're here!" Papa said, stopping suddenly and dismounting. He helped Mama and Anna off their horse, then came for Elsa.

Where was "here"?

Papa stood in the middle of a grassy area covered with mossy boulders stacked in strange formations. Stone steps led down to the center of the area, as if there had been something there once upon a time. Steam eerily seeped from hidden geysers all around them. Wherever "here" was, it seemed mysterious. Mama looked more worried than Elsa had ever seen her before. *This is my fault,* Elsa thought.

"Elsa, come here," Papa said, and she ran into his arms. "It will be all right." They were the first words he had said to her since they had been in the Great Hall. Mama was close behind, holding Anna in her arms. "Please!" Papa called into the darkness. "Help! It's my daughter!"

Who was Papa talking to? Elsa was about to ask him when she noticed the boulders beginning to rock, then roll down the steps, headed directly for them.

Elsa pulled at Mama's leg, burying her face in her dress. Papa pulled the three of them closer as the boulders moved in. Elsa peeked out from her mother's dress.

All at once, the boulders stopped moving, and up sprang dozens of small trolls. They looked as if they were chiseled from stone. The moss that had grown on their backs looked like garments, and different-colored crystals hung from their necks. They had small tufts of mossy green hair on top of their heads and large ears, and the whites of their close-set eyes glowed in the moonlight. The trolls reminded Elsa of hedgehogs.

"It's the king!" one of the trolls cried as they shuffled forward. A troll with a long mossy cape moved to the front of the pack. He had an intricate beaded necklace. "Make way for Grand Pabbie!"

"Your Majesty." Grand Pabbie bowed his head. He reached for Elsa's hand. "Born with the powers or cursed?"

Elsa inhaled sharply. How did he know?

Papa seemed to be thinking the same thing. "Born," he said, sounding nervous. "And they're getting stronger."

Grand Pabbie motioned to Mama. She kneeled down and held Anna out to him, and he put his hand on Anna's head. His bushy eyebrows furrowed. "You are lucky it wasn't her heart. The heart is not so easily changed." He shrugged. "But the head can be persuaded."

Papa looked at Mama in surprise. "Do what you must," he told Grand Pabbie.

"I recommend we remove all magic, even memories of magic, to be safe," Grand Pabbie said.

Remove all magic? "But she won't remember I have powers?" Elsa asked, unable to keep quiet.

"It's for the best," Papa said, touching her shoulder.

Elsa's circle of people she could trust was small already. If Anna didn't remember she could do magic, who could she share the burden with? Her heart started to beat faster. Anna was her fiercest ally. Her baking partner. Her sister. They couldn't keep secrets from each other.

"Listen to me, Elsa," Grand Pabbie said gently, as if he had heard her thoughts. "Your power will only grow." He raised his hands to the sky and blue images filled the air. They turned into the outlines of people and a girl.

The girl conjured up the most beautiful snowflake Elsa had ever seen. "There is beauty in it, but also great danger."

The snowflake turned bright red and burst.

Elsa's eyes widened.

"You must learn to control it," Grand Pabbie told her. "Fear will be your enemy."

The people's outlines turned red while the girl in the middle stayed blue. Elsa could sense the girl's fear. Was this meant to be her destiny? Would she be an outcast? The red crowds closed in on the girl. Elsa heard a scream, and the image shattered. She hid her face in her father's chest.

"No!" Papa said, and looked at Mama. "We'll protect her. She can learn to control it. I'm sure. We'll keep her powers hidden from everyone." He looked at Elsa and paused. "Including Anna."

"No! Please, no!" Elsa begged. This was too much. "I won't hurt her again. I promise." She looked at Mama.

"This isn't a punishment, darling," her mother said. "You heard your father and Grand Pabbie. We must protect both of you."

Elsa couldn't believe it. She didn't want Anna not to know the true her. Anna believed in her gift. Other than her parents, Anna was the only one she could share it with. Who would she make snow with? Without Anna, a gift like this wasn't much fun at all.

"She will be safe this way, Elsa," Grand Pabbie reminded her. "You both will be."

Elsa tried to think of something that would change their minds, but she couldn't even get her parents' attention. They were focused on Anna. Elsa watched in agony as Grand Pabbie touched Anna's head, then swept his hand into the air.

Papa patted Elsa's back. "I know this is hard, but you're a brave girl. You want what's best for Anna, don't you?"

"Yes," Elsa said, but she was also thinking, *I need Anna. She's the only one who understands.* "Yes, but Anna is the only one I can share my gift with. Don't take that away."

"You'll be fine, Elsa," her father promised.

There was a whistling, like the sound of wind, and then an icy blue cloud formed above their heads. It reminded Elsa of her own magic. She watched as images of her and Anna flashed by: the two of them playing in the snow in the Great Hall, ice-skating across its floor, and building Olaf . . . all the things they'd done that would have been impossible without magic. How had Grand Pabbie been able to pull those memories out of her sister's head?

Just as quickly, the memories of her and Anna changed. The Great Hall moment turned into one of Anna sledding outside. The two of them ice-skating indoors became an excursion on a nearby pond, and their time with Olaf indoors morphed into a scene of them building a snowman in the forest. Their memories were being erased. It was more than Elsa could bear.

"No, please!" Elsa cried, feeling the warmth tingle in her fingertips. A blue glow hovered above her hands.

"Don't worry. I will leave the fun," Grand Pabbie promised.

But it wasn't about fun. It was about the two of them sharing a gift Elsa had been given. And now the leader of the trolls was taking it away. Elsa watched in agony as Grand Pabbie swirled the images into a ball, just as she usually conjured snow. His hands slowly moved toward Anna's head. Elsa already knew what would happen. When Grand Pabbie touched her, the new memories would replace the old ones. Anna and Elsa's bond would be lost forever. Elsa couldn't let that happen.

"No!" she cried, pulling from her father's embrace.

Her hand connected with Grand Pabbie's just as his fingers grazed Anna's forehead.

"Elsa, no!" Papa cried as Mama reached for her in a panic. But it was too late.

An explosion of light vibrated off the boulders around them. Rocks began to crumble and fall from the mountains the valley was nestled between. The trolls ran for cover. The light grew brighter and brighter till it burst into what seemed like a million little stars. It was the last thing Elsa saw before her world faded to black.

CHAPTER FOURTEEN

Elsa

Elsa awoke from the vivid memory, gasping for air as if she'd been underwater too long. She inhaled deeply, trying hard to remember to keep breathing.

"Elsa! Elsa!" Olaf was standing over her. "You collapsed! Are you okay?"

Someone was pounding on her bedroom door. "Princess Elsa! Princess Elsa! Are you all right?"

It was Hans.

"Why isn't she answering?" she heard him shout.

"Princess?" It was Lord Peterssen. "Can you hear us?"

"Yes!" Elsa called out, her voice sounding shaky. "I will be right there."

How long had she been out?

"Elsa, what happened?" Olaf asked.

Elsa sat up, her whole body feeling like jelly. The memory cut like a knife. Her powers weren't new; her parents had known she'd possessed them all along, but somehow she'd forgotten them. The pain of that truth and what had happened almost overwhelmed her. "Anna was my sister," she choked out. "My magic killed her."

CHAPTER FIFTEEN

Anna

Anna's cheeks were flushed with excitement.

It was coronation day!

The bakery was packed. Even though most people she knew wouldn't travel to Arendelle to see Princess Elsa's coronation in person, Harmon was still celebrating in its own way. Many people were closing their shops early and planning to rejoice in the streets with shared food, good friends, and dancing. Ma had baked several cakes for the occasion, Goran from the market was bringing a roasted pig and potatoes, and Papa had talked with some men who were bringing their lutes. It was a glorious summer day, and she could feel the charge in the air.

After three years without a true leader, Arendelle was finally getting its queen.

Coronation day was all about new beginnings and fresh starts. Anna wished the day when she, too, would get her new beginning could arrive sooner rather than later, but how could she argue with her parents? She was still young. Sort of. And they needed her help. Definitely. Three more years would go by fast . . . she hoped.

"Thank you, Anna!" Mrs. Eriksen said as Anna placed several cinnamon buns in a bag for her. "I will see you later at the party."

"See you tonight!" Anna said, watching Mrs. Eriksen open the bakery door. When it opened, Anna noticed a young man outside with a reindeer. Their backs were to the door. Kristoff!

She couldn't believe he had come. She wiped her hands on her apron and rushed outside, hearing Kristoff's conversation with Sven in the process.

"Yes, I'm going to talk to her. Maybe." Kristoff huffed. "You, Bulda, Grand Pabbie . . . you act like this is so easy! They may be so-called love experts, but they've never left the valley."

Sven snorted.

"Hi," Anna interrupted, feeling funny. She was suddenly very aware of how she looked, and how he did, too. Kristoff had on a bright blue dress shirt and clean pants. She was wearing a green dress under a flour-and-icing-covered apron. Her braids, which she'd had in for two days, needed refreshing. "Were you looking for me? I mean, not actually looking, but you're here, so maybe . . . you're hungry?"

He immediately blushed. "What? Yes. I mean, no. I . . ." He pressed a bunch of carrots into her hands. "I just wanted to give you what I owed you."

"Oh." Anna looked down. "You didn't have to bring me back—*oof!*"

Sven had bumped into Anna, sending her flying into Kristoff's arms. The two tumbled backward, falling onto several stacks of flour Anna's parents hadn't had a chance to bring into the shop yet.

"This is awkward," Anna said, struggling to get up. "Not because you're awkward. Because we're . . . I'm . . . awkward." She stood up. "You're gorgeous. Wait, what?"

She'd never said anything like that before. Did she think Kristoff was gorgeous? She needed to change the subject fast. "So that's the only reason you came by? To give me carrots?"

"Oh. Uh . . ." Kristoff looked like a reindeer caught in carriage lights. "Uh . . ." Sven kept snorting. "I can't stay. I have a delivery in Arendelle, so I'm headed down the mountain."

"Down the mountain?" Anna cut in. "That's where I'm going! Well, not today, but in three years. I'm going to open up my own bakery in Arendelle."

Kristoff scratched his head. "In three years?"

"Yes," Anna said. "My parents want me to run their shop, but I want to leave Harmon someday." Kristoff just looked at her. "You should understand. You get to see the whole kingdom with your ice business! Your carriage takes you everywhere, while I'm always stuck here."

"I wouldn't call it *stuck*," Kristoff muttered. "Seems like a nice place to live. Try begging to sleep in people's barns all the time when you're on the road and being raised in a field full of rocks."

"What?" Anna thought she must have heard him incorrectly.

"Nothing." Kristoff looked away.

Anna thought again of the life Freya had lost. She didn't want to waste another moment being in a place she didn't truly love. "You don't understand." She played with one of her braids. *Three years feels so far away.*

"Hey." Kristoff moved closer. "Your hair."

"Oh." She was used to this question. "The white stripe? I was born with it," she explained. "That's what my parents were told. They actually adopted me when I was a baby. I dreamt that I was kissed by a troll."

Kristoff's eyes widened. "Did you say 'troll'?" He hurried after her to hear more.

CHAPTER SIXTEEN

Elsa

"Anna is . . . dead?" Olaf repeated as if he didn't understand the words coming out of his mouth.

Elsa saw his heartbroken face and heard a sob escape her lips before she even realized it was happening. "I think I killed her."

A blue glow appeared above her fingers, ice escaping and climbing up the walls and covering the floor. The world waited outside her door, pounding harder to get in. The ice couldn't have come at a worse time, but Elsa was too consumed with grief to care who saw it now.

Anna was dead. That was why her parents had hidden her sister's existence from her. No wonder Mama had always looked so forlorn. Elsa had changed the footprint of their family forever. How could her parents forgive her for what she had done? How could the kingdom?

Wait.

Elsa stopped crying and thought of the fountain in the courtyard and their family portrait in the hallway. Both showed a family of three. Wouldn't her parents and Mr. Ludenburg want to keep Anna's memory alive by including her in such works of art? Wouldn't people talk about the lost princess? Why would her parents have hidden a painting of their original family in Elsa's lockbox? Yet no one had ever uttered a word about Anna before. In fact, Mama had always told people who asked that she couldn't have any other children after Elsa.

"This doesn't make sense," Elsa said, her questions coming faster. She felt her heart quicken and heard a whooshing in her ears. She was missing something, but what? "I know people have always tried to protect me, but how could Mama and Papa make the whole kingdom forget I had a sister?"

"I don't know," Olaf said, toddling over. "Maybe this letter will explain it. When you dropped the painting, this was underneath it."

Elsa looked up in surprise. "Letter?"

Olaf held a piece of parchment in his twig hand. Elsa recognized the handwriting immediately.

It was Mama's.

"Elsa!" Lord Peterssen and Hans were both calling to her now, pounding on the door again. "Elsa, are you all right? Answer us!"

Elsa didn't answer. Fingers trembling, she reached for the letter in Olaf's outstretched hand just as she heard a key jingling in her door. Her heart pounding, she skimmed the letter quickly. There was no time to read it carefully. Instead, she searched for the answer she most needed to find. Her eyes passed over words and phrases like *trolls, the Valley of the Living Rock,* and *a secret we've hidden for years,* and she kept searching till she found what she was looking for.

We love you and your sister very much, but circumstance forced us to keep you apart.

Keep us apart? Did that mean Anna was alive?

Elsa started to laugh and cry at the same time.

She was not alone. She had a sister!

"Olaf! She's alive! Anna's alive!" Elsa said as the commotion outside her door increased.

Olaf's face broke into a toothy grin. "Where is she? We have to find her!"

"I know! I know!" Elsa looked down at the letter again, prepared to actually read it this time and learn how this was possible. *Our darling Elsa, if you're reading this, we're gone. Otherwise—*

Her bedroom door flew open.

The letter slipped from Elsa's hands as Olaf dove for the dressing area. Hans rushed into the room.

"Elsa!" he said, his face filled with fear. "What happened? Are you all right?"

"I'm fine!" Elsa insisted, pushing Hans out the door as he, Lord Peterssen, Gerda, and the Duke attempted to enter. She moved into the hallway, shut the door behind her, and realized Kai and Olina were also there. Elsa wondered: were they in on the secret, too? Did they know about Anna and where she was? She had so many new questions that needed answers.

Lord Peterssen clutched his chest. "We thought you were hurt."

"No," Elsa said, laughing despite herself. "I'm fine. I'm better than fine. Truly."

"Why wouldn't you answer us?" Hans pleaded. "We thought . . ."

The Duke looked sharply at Elsa over his spectacles. "We thought you were running away from Prince Hans's proposal."

"Proposal?" Elsa repeated, and then she remembered all at once what they had been discussing before she heard Olaf's crash and hurried back inside her room. "I . . ."

She needed to read that letter. What circumstances

forced her parents to separate their daughters? Why didn't she learn about her powers until her parents' death? Why didn't the rest of the kingdom talk about Anna? If her sister was alive, where was she? Had Elsa frightened her away with her magic?

She needed to read the letter immediately.

"Yes, Prince Hans is waiting for an answer," said the Duke, motioning to a confused Hans.

"I think this conversation should wait till after the coronation," Hans said.

"Yes, we need to go to the chapel," Lord Peterssen reminded the Duke.

Gerda placed a hand on Elsa's arm. "Princess, you look flushed."

"Hans, I . . ." Elsa looked from the prince to the others. All she could think about was Mama's letter. "I need another moment." She reached for the door handle. The Duke held the door closed.

"I think you've spent enough time shutting people out," he said firmly. "Don't you?"

Elsa felt a flash of anger at the Duke's words.

"You can't talk to the princess like that," Hans said. The two started arguing.

Elsa looked desperately back at her door. A letter with keys to her past was on one side, while Hans and the Duke were trying to decide her future on the other. Her fingertips started to tingle, and this time she couldn't hold her emotions back. She needed to get to that letter.

"I'm not doing this right now," Elsa said shakily, and the Duke tried to interrupt her again. "Now if you'll excuse me."

The Duke touched her arm. "Princess, if I may—"

The tremors going through her body came in waves. Her high collar was beginning to itch terribly, and her emotions were too strong to control. "No, you may not," Elsa snapped. "I need to go back to my room. You should leave."

"Leave?" The Duke looked outraged. "Before the coronation?"

"Princess, there is no time to go back to your room again," Lord Peterssen pleaded.

"The priest is waiting," Kai added.

"Princess?" Gerda said, sounding unsure. "Are you all right?"

No, she wasn't all right. She needed to read that letter. *Circumstance forced us to keep you apart.* She needed to find Anna. They'd been separated for far too long. Elsa looked from the crowd in front of her to her door again. If they wouldn't let her enter, she'd find another way back inside. The castle had many secret passages. She'd go around. Elsa tried pushing her way through the crowd in desperation. Her sleeves felt so tight; she could barely move her arms.

"Elsa, wait." Hans reached for her, accidentally pulling off one of her gloves.

"Give me my glove!" Elsa panicked.

Hans held it out of reach. "Something is troubling you. Please just talk to me," he said. "Let me help you."

"Princess! The priest is waiting," Lord Peterssen said.

"Weselton is a close trade partner and I should be at the coronation . . ." the Duke was muttering.

Gerda tried to intervene. "The princess is upset."

Elsa closed her eyes. "Enough," she whispered.

The Duke kept talking. "I was trying to help you present yourself in the best possible light after closing yourself away and . . ."

Elsa needed him to stop talking. All she could hear inside her head was Mama's words.

We love you and your sister very much.

Sister.

Sister.

She had a sister!

Nothing else mattered. She pushed past them and ran down the hall. The voices followed.

"Princess, wait!" Kai cried.

Elsa was done waiting. She needed to read that letter. *Sister. Sister.* Her breathing became ragged and her fingers tingled so badly they burned.

"Princess Elsa!" Hans called.

"I said, enough!"

Ice flew away from her hands with such force it shot across the floor, spiking into jagged, twisted icicles that formed an immediate barrier between her and the others. Hans jumped out of the way of a spike that threatened to hit him in the chest. The Duke was knocked off his feet. Frozen crystals of ice floated through the air and silently fell to the floor.

Elsa gasped in horror.

Her secret was a secret no more.

"Sorcery," she heard the Duke whisper. His face pulsed with anger as he struggled to stand up. "So that's why. I knew something dubious was going on here!"

Elsa grasped her own hand in shock. She locked eyes with Hans and saw his confusion.

"Elsa?" he whispered.

She did the only thing she still could do: run.

Down the hall she raced, bursting through the closest set of doors she could find.

"There she is!" someone cried.

Without realizing it, Elsa had exited the castle. She was standing in the courtyard in front of the statue of her and her parents, where hundreds of people were waiting. When they saw her, the people began to clap and cheer.

Elsa started to back up, then heard voices. Hans, Kai, the Duke, and Lord Peterssen were coming. With no choice, she ran down the steps, holding up her coronation gown as she darted into the crowd.

"It is her!" someone shouted.

"Princess Elsa!" People bowed to her.

Elsa spun around, looking for a path out of the crowd.

A man blocked her. "Our future queen!"

Elsa's heart was pounding. She tried to go another way.

A woman holding a baby stepped forward. "Your Royal Highness," she said kindly.

Elsa immediately thought of her mother and Anna.

"Are you all right?" the woman asked.

"No," Elsa whispered, her eyes darting left and right as she backed up again. She bumped into the fountain with the family statue behind her and put out her hands to stop herself. Instantly, the water in the fountain froze. The geyser that was shooting high into the sky crystalized in midair, as if it were reaching out to grab her.

The villagers shrieked.

"There she is!" she heard the Duke shout from the castle steps. "Stop her!"

Elsa saw Hans and Lord Peterssen and hesitated. Hans was her safety net, but she couldn't risk hurting him. She couldn't risk hurting anyone. She thought about which way to run, but people were on all sides of her. Didn't they realize? She couldn't control what she was doing. She needed to be alone.

"Please, just stay away from me. Stay away!"

More snow shot straight from her hands and hit the castle steps, exploding with such force it froze them. The motion knocked the Duke off his feet again, sending his glasses flying. Elsa was breathing hard in shock.

The Duke sat up, reaching for his glasses. "Monster. *Monster!*" he shouted.

She wasn't. She didn't want to hurt a soul. She looked around for someone who understood her, but there was no one. Her people looked terrified. Even the kind woman now seemed to be shielding her baby from Elsa.

Sister.

Anna had once known that Elsa had the ability to do magic. Surely, Anna would be able to understand her again. Elsa had to find her at all costs.

Elsa started to run again and didn't stop till she cleared the castle courtyard and reached the village.

"Elsa!" she heard Hans calling. "Elsa!"

But she kept running. She spotted the steps leading down to the water and descended them, running until there was nothing but water in front of her. There was nowhere left to go. She stepped back as she saw Hans approaching, and her foot landed in the water. Instantly, the water froze beneath her shoe. She looked down in wonder as tiny crystals of ice spread. The wind started to whip up and snow began to fall as she took another step. The ice spread again, forming a pathway for her escape. She took it.

"Wait, please!" Hans begged, running after her with Lord Peterssen on his trail. The snow was falling harder. "Elsa, stop!"

Elsa wouldn't stop now. Finding her sister was more important than anything in the world. All thoughts of her coronation slipped away. Elsa took a deep breath and continued onto the ice, praying it wouldn't crack beneath her feet. The ice held firm, spreading as she ran across it. Her cape billowing around her, Elsa felt resolve coursing through her veins as she took off across the fjord into the gathering darkness.

CHAPTER SEVENTEEN

Anna

Suddenly, there was a rumbling beneath Kristoff and Anna's feet. A flock of birds shot by overhead. Sven started snorting and shuffling as a family of squirrels scurried past them across the street. Anna heard someone shriek and saw an elk run past. Sven tore off.

"Sven!" Kristoff shouted.

Anna and Kristoff chased Sven into the village square. People had started coming out of their homes and shops to see what was going on. Birds and animals began streaming out of the woods in every direction.

"What's happening?" Anna asked as the rumbling grew louder.

The sun vanished behind the clouds, and a cold wind whipped through the trees, causing them to sway.

"Look!" someone shouted, pointing down the mountain.

It was one of the finest summer days Anna could remember, but the fjord somehow appeared to be freezing over. A blue glow hovered above the water as it froze, knocking the boats in the harbor sideways. Suddenly, the freeze began to trickle up the mountainside, heading right toward them.

"Ice," Kristoff whispered.

Anna didn't understand what was happening, but she knew they had to get out of the way of whatever was coming. "We need to warn the others. Quickly!" Anna yelled. "Sven!"

Sven ran straight toward her. Anna jumped onto his back.

"Hey! Wait for me!" Kristoff ran after them. "Go, Sven! Through the village!"

"Take cover!" Anna shouted as the blue glow grew closer, ice trailing along right behind it, threatening to overtake them. "Everyone get inside!" Kristoff finally caught up with them and jumped onto Sven's back behind Anna.

People began running as the wind whipped up. The temperature plummeted and the sky became completely gray. Suddenly, there was a whooshing sound. Sven stopped short, throwing Kristoff and Anna off him as the blue haze washed over them and kept going. Anna and Kristoff struggled to stand up as the ice crackled and spread under their feet as a squall seemed to draw up around them, filling the sky with snow.

Anna didn't even realize she and Kristoff had been holding on to each other. She kept waiting for the freak storm to pass, but instead, now it was snowing. In the middle of the summer. Her heart pounded hard. *What is going on in Arendelle?*

Three days later, Anna was still wondering.

For the past seventy-two hours she'd watched the scene outside her window. Blinding snow and ice covered the rooftops, blanketed the ground, and piled high in snowdrifts. Ice crackled and formed giant icicles that threatened to topple off rooftops and crash to the ground.

"We stay inside," Papa told Anna and Ma as a fierce wind blew outside their bakery door. "We keep the fire going as long as possible and we bake as much as we can. We need the food. Who knows how long this weather will continue?"

Even with a fire raging, the house felt colder than Anna remembered it ever being in winter.

"It is good you moved the chickens and the animals into the barn, but it still must be awfully cold," Ma said, rubbing her arms to keep warm.

Anna stared out the window. The streets were deserted. Snow was drifting higher in front of doorways despite people's best efforts to keep it from piling up. They needed a way out of their homes in an emergency, but Anna couldn't help wondering where they would go in weather like this. They'd freeze to death.

"It's awfully crowded now with the animals and that ice delivery boy staying in the barn with his reindeer."

Anna looked up. "Kristoff doesn't mind. He likes sleeping in barns," she joked.

Ma looked at her curiously. "You two know each other?"

Anna looked out the window again and tried not to let her mother see her blush. "A little. I wish he would come inside."

Papa threw another log onto the fire. Their pile of kindling was getting dangerously low. They'd have to go out and cut down more soon. "I asked him to, but he won't leave his reindeer."

"I don't understand," Anna said. "How could it snow like this in the middle of the summer?" Her gut told her something or someone had caused it. "Is Arendelle cursed?"

Ma and Papa looked at each other.

"There's no such thing as curses, right?" Anna pressed. Why did she think they knew something they weren't telling her?

There was a heavy pounding at the door, and Papa and Ma looked at each other again. Papa rushed to the window and peered out. "Let them in! Quickly!"

Ma opened the door, the snow and wind practically overtaking her as she struggled to hold the door for their visitors. Two men were bundled up from head to toe in hats, gloves, and layers of scarves. Still, they were shivering.

"The snow is getting deeper," said Goran, unwrapping a scarf from around his face. "Soon it will cover rooftops if it keeps falling."

"That's impossible," Ma said, quickly handing him a hot mug of glogg. "It has never snowed that much."

Mr. Larsen looked grim. "I believe we are cursed."

"See!" Anna agreed, and her parents looked awkward.

"Did you not see how it came from Arendelle and traveled up the mountain?" Mr. Larsen continued. "How else do you explain snow like this in the middle of the summer? Something happened at Princess Elsa's coronation. I am sure of it!"

"No one from Arendelle has come to bring news of the princess or what has happened," Goran agreed. "For all we know, we could have lost her in this weather."

Princess Elsa was their future. Anna was pinning her hopes to her. "I'm sure she's fine. Right, Ma?"

Ma was looking at Papa. "Surely the princess is safe. She

is probably busy preparing the kingdom for this unforeseen blizzard."

Anna looked out the window again, straining to see her beloved Arendelle, but the mountainside was covered in a sheet of ice and there were whiteout conditions. Arendelle looked as if it had disappeared.

"Then why send no word to all the villages?" Goran asked. "Wouldn't the castle come to tell us what is happening? We can't continue like this. We are running out of firewood. The crops we planted must surely be dead by now, and we will have nothing to store for the real winter still to come. We aren't prepared for these conditions."

"In a few weeks' time, we will run out of food," Mr. Larsen added grimly. "The fjord appears to be frozen over, so no ships can get in or out to send for help. The horses will not last long outside in this weather. We are done for."

The situation was direr than Anna had realized. "Papa, someone needs to get to Arendelle and find out what is going on."

Papa put his hand on her shoulder and attempted a smile, but it was weak at best. "Why don't you go to the bakery and make sure the fire is still burning while Ma gets everyone more glogg?"

"Papa—" Anna tried to interrupt, but he cut her off.

"Go ahead now," he said softly. "Don't worry."

"Listen to Papa," Ma agreed.

Anna walked slowly to the kitchen. She looked back, hearing the men and Ma talking quietly by the fire. It popped and crackled even as a breeze blew through cracks in the walls. *Curses*. Was such a thing possible? Ma and Papa seemed to know something they weren't saying, but Anna was with Mr. Larsen: there was something unnatural about the weather and the way the ice had traveled up the mountain. Anna had never witnessed anything like that before. Maybe curses were real. But why was someone or something threatening to destroy their kingdom? How much longer would they be able to survive like this?

Not long at all.

One thing was certain: someone had to get to Arendelle and find answers fast.

Papa was in no condition to journey to the castle and get help. Goran and Mr. Larsen were also older. Would they even be able to make it down the mountain? They needed someone skilled at traveling in conditions such as those. Someone who was skilled at handling ice.

Kristoff.

Anna looked back at the others again. No one noticed her standing near the doorway to the bakery. They didn't see her quietly go upstairs and search her armoire for her warmest hat, cloak, and gloves. They wouldn't find the note explaining why she had left until they came to her room looking for her. And they were too engrossed in their conversation to notice her slip through the bakery doorway and gather supplies of water, bread, and whatever vegetables she could find. Without a word, she pulled open the door, determined to help her people. She was almost blown back by the wind. Anna was shocked at how cold her exposed face felt, but she kept going, holding on to railings and overturned carts as she slowly made her way to the barn.

When she arrived, she found Kristoff playing his lute for Sven and the other animals, who were all huddled around a small fire. He saw her and dropped his instrument in surprise.

"What are you doing out in this weather?" he asked.

Anna's teeth were chattering. She rubbed her arms to keep warm. "I want you to take me to Arendelle."

He sighed and picked up his lute. "I don't take people places."

"Let me rephrase that." She threw the bag of supplies at him.

"Hey!" He winced and rubbed his shoulder.

"Sorry!" She stepped closer, holding her ground. "Take me down the mountain. Please."

Sven nudged the bag, and Kristoff opened it. Inside were some carrots, rope, and an ice ax. He looked at her curiously.

"Look, we need to figure out how to stop this winter. You saw it yourself—the ice started in Arendelle. We need to know what happened down there at the coronation that caused this. It feels . . . magical." Kristoff didn't laugh at her suggestion, so she kept talking. "We need to find out what's going on and figure out how to protect the kingdom."

Kristoff pulled his hat over his eyes. "We leave at dawn."

She took a horse blanket off a barn stall and threw it at him. It hit Kristoff in the face. "Sorry! Sorry! I'm sorry. I didn't . . ." She cleared her throat. There was no more time to waste. "We leave now. Right now."

Anna was going to Arendelle. It wasn't the way she had planned to make the journey, but she was going all the same. She thought again in wonder of the frozen castle and the princess. Her gut told her someone down there needed her. Anna could feel it in her bones.

CHAPTER EIGHTEEN

Elsa

Elsa's mind was swirling as fast as the snow that fell around her in thick sheets. She'd run across the fjord, the water beneath her feet freezing as hard as glass with each step. She headed deep into the forest and didn't stop till the moon was overhead. Faster and faster she asked her legs to carry her, away from the castle, the village, and the only life she'd ever known.

Anna was alive.

Nothing was more important than finding her.

A cold wind whipped her purple cape in front of her face, blocking Elsa's view. She pushed it aside, trying to get her bearings. She didn't know where she was, but it didn't matter. She had to keep going so she wasn't followed.

Another gust of wind sent her sideways. The howling whistle sounded like voices.

Monster! Monster!

The Duke's words echoed inside her head. It was coronation day, but instead of being crowned queen, she had revealed her powers and fled Arendelle. The kingdom was hidden under a deep freeze she had somehow caused. But how? Her magic allowed her to create ice. Could it also change the weather? The idea was awe-inspiring and worrisome at the same time. It was the middle of the summer. People weren't prepared for snow. How would they manage? Were they frightened?

Elsa thought again of that mother shielding her baby from her. *Monster.* Was that what her people thought of her now that they knew the truth? She remembered Lord Peterssen's face when ice had grown around him like daggers. Hans had looked equally astonished when a blue glow appeared above her hands and snow blasted into the room. She could only imagine what the Duke of Weselton was saying about her to anyone who would listen. They'd all thought they knew her. The truth was no one did.

Would Anna?

That was when it dawned on her: Did Anna know she was a princess of Arendelle? Or had she been kept in the dark, as Elsa had been? Why was Anna's existence a secret in the first place? Her parents had obviously wanted her to find out about Anna, or they wouldn't have hidden that canvas and letter in her lockbox. Why were they being kept apart?

How could I have left without that letter? Elsa cursed herself again. *And Olaf!* What if someone found Olaf in her room? Her heart started to beat wildly at the thought. A blue glow appeared above her fingertips. She shook out her hands and tried to concentrate. *No!* She couldn't let her powers control her.

The only way to save Olaf and retrieve the letter was to go back to the castle. Elsa turned toward home—or at least she thought she did. Arendelle was obscured by the blinding snow. She couldn't find her way back if she tried.

And even if she did . . . *Monster.* That was what the Duke had called her. What if Lord Peterssen and the advisors agreed with him? She'd be sent to the dungeons. She'd lose her crown. She'd never find Anna.

Just breathe, she reminded herself, and the blue glow above her hands disappeared.

Olaf was a pro when it came to hiding. Over the past few years, they'd worked out a number of places in her room for him to disappear to if anyone came calling. Now if he just heard a voice outside her door, he'd spring into action. Besides, no one had entered her room since her parents died. Chances were they weren't going to look in her room now, either. Hopefully Olaf had heard the commotion, grabbed the letter, and hid. When things calmed down, she'd find a way to go back for him. Olaf knew she'd never abandon him. That just left the problem of the missing letter.

Think, Elsa, she willed herself. *What do you remember reading?* She'd been so excited she'd only skimmed it the first time, looking for what was most important: proof that Anna existed. But she had noted a few other phrases. There was something written about trolls. That made sense. In her vision, she'd seen a large group of trolls and their leader, called Grand Pabbie. The family had traveled far by horse to find him, crossing a river and climbing into the mountains to a valley. The mountain range ahead of her was remote and imposing. Maybe that was where Grand Pabbie was! In the distance, the rocky face of the North Mountain loomed, large and impressive. Even in the summer, the peak was covered with snow. Few had attempted to climb it, which meant no one would follow her up there. The mountain was a kingdom of isolation, and it looked like she was the queen. She'd keep going in that direction until she found the trolls or her legs gave out. She wasn't even tired. And the cold never bothered her, anyway.

For two days, Elsa trudged through the snow to reach the base of the North Mountain. It was a feat she hadn't been sure she could manage, but when she finally arrived, she had a bigger problem. She might not have been cold, but she definitely didn't have the equipment to climb a rocky facade. Or did she?

No one could see her at that altitude. She didn't have to conceal her powers in the middle of the wilderness. After having been locked away in her room, hiding her secret from the world, she was suddenly free to use her magic in a way she never had before. All her practice had led her to that moment: what could she create to help her move mountains?

Elsa looked down at her hands. She was wearing only one glove. Her gloves had served as "protection" from her powers for far too long. It was time to let go. She pulled the glove off and let it fly into the wind. She was finally free.

Lifting her hand to the sky, she concentrated on creating a giant snowflake that crystallized in midair and floated away. Then she lifted her other hand and made another snowflake, watching it fly away as well. Pulse racing, Elsa kept building, her face breaking into a smile as she realized the possibilities were endless. Here she could really use her gift and see what she was capable of.

A blue glow circled her swirling arms as she imagined crystals that immediately froze and shattered into snow. *Think bigger,* Elsa resolved as she shot a stream of ice up the

mountainside. *What else can I do?* she wondered. *Anything.*
Everything I can think of! She'd never felt so alive.

Elsa kept shooting snow into the air as she ran closer to
the base of the North Mountain, stopping short when she
stared into a gorge with a hundred-foot drop. Once more,
her cape caught on the wind, hitting her in the face. The
item served no purpose on a mountaintop. Elsa unclipped
the brooch holding it closed and let the cape fly off the
side of the mountain, disappearing into the darkness. The
gorge was a different problem. It had to be almost thirty feet
across. It was impossible to jump, but with powers like hers,
why did she need to worry about jumping?

For so long she had feared anyone's knowing she had
powers, but in her recovered memories, her family looked
at them as a gift. Now she could see why: look at what
she could create with her two hands! If she used to make
winter wonderlands in the castle for Anna, why couldn't
she create an ice palace on a mountaintop? *Let your fears
go,* she reminded herself. She imagined a staircase of ice
connecting both sides of the gorge. Was it possible? What
about a staircase that carried her up the entire mountain?

Anything was possible if she believed in her powers like
Anna once had.

Elsa took a deep breath and backed up a few paces
before running across the snowy peak. *Staircase,* she

thought as her hands shot out in front of her, forming several icy steps that climbed into the air. She paused for a split second before gingerly stepping onto the first one. The stairs were so sturdy she ran up them, throwing her hands out over and over, creating steps that led her all the way to the peak of the North Mountain. Her mind and her fingertips somehow worked in perfect harmony to create exactly what she needed at exactly the right moment.

When Elsa finally reached the top, she didn't find any trolls, but the view was breathtaking. Few mountaineers had climbed to such heights, and there she was, high over the entire kingdom. Arendelle was far in the distance, as tiny as a speck. Even if she hadn't found the trolls yet, the North Mountain felt like a good place for her to recharge and figure out how to find Anna. She'd build a palace as stunning as the landscape to shelter in. One that reflected the new her. Mama had called her powers a gift, hadn't she? Well, they were. And there was no reason to conceal them from the world at the top of a mountain.

Elsa stomped her foot into the snow, creating a giant snowflake that unfurled under her. The snowflake multiplied again and again, forming the footprint for her new home. Next she imagined her fortress rising into the air, and it did just that, the frozen wonder growing and expanding. This time, the ice didn't form sharp, jagged daggers. She created ornate columns and archways more exquisite than even those found in Arendelle Castle. Elsa filled in every detail she could think of for her home, until she created the peaks that would be her roof. For a final touch, Elsa made a giant snowflake that burst into the most intricate chandelier she could imagine.

Standing inside her creation, Elsa knew there was still something missing. She had created a new look for her life, but hadn't done a thing to change her own appearance. Pulling at her uncomfortable hairstyle, she let several loose tendrils frame her face. Next, she took out the tight bun, and her braided hair hung down her back. Elsa didn't stop there. This gown had weighed her down for too long. It was time for it to go as well. With a wave of her hands, she imagined a new dress that suited her personality and style. Something light and freeing. Ice crystallized over the bottom of her teal dress, forming a new one that was a shimmering pale blue. Gone were the itchy high collar and the annoying long sleeves that restricted her movements. Her new gown was strapless, her neck was open, and her arms were loosely wrapped in silk. A light sheer cape was made up of a pattern of snowflakes as unique as she was.

By the time she was finished creating her fortress and a new look, the sun was beginning to rise over the mountains.

Elsa stepped out onto one of her balconies and reveled at the majesty of her new kingdom.

Anna would like it here, Elsa thought with satisfaction.

She just had to find her.

Looking out over the snow and the ice, Elsa tried to imagine where Grand Pabbie and the trolls might be. If they weren't hidden at the top of the North Mountain, where were they? She drummed her fingers on the icy railing of the balcony and thought again of her vision. The night Papa and Mama had taken them up into the mountains to find the trolls, Papa had held on to a map.

Think, Elsa. What was he looking for? Where did we go? It was some sort of valley.

The Valley of the Living Rock! She'd spotted that name in the letter. That had to be where Grand Pabbie was hidden. Based on how long it had taken to reach the North Mountain, Elsa had to guess the Valley of the Living Rock was at least a day's walk from there, and she would have to go back down the mountain to find it. She yawned despite herself. It had been days since she'd rested. She needed sleep, but when she woke, she'd begin another journey— one that would lead her to her sister.

CHAPTER NINETEEN

Anna

"This is really nice!" Anna exclaimed as she climbed onto the bench next to Kristoff and admired his sleigh.

The sled was far superior to the one her papa had. The upper half of Kristoff's sleigh was shiny dark wood, while the lower part was hand-painted black and red, with beige triangles outlining the rim. The pattern reminded her of teeth. It was clear this sleigh was not to be messed with. Anna threw her sack in the back, and it landed next to Kristoff's reddish lute, his sack, and some mountaineering equipment.

"Careful!" Kristoff barked. "You almost broke my lute."

"Sorry!" Anna winced. "Didn't know you were bringing your *lute* with you on this trip. I'm not sure you'll really have time to play the next few days."

Kristoff gave her a look. "I only have it in the sleigh because I carry all of Sven's and my belongings in here. We just paid the sled off, so I don't need you breaking anything."

"Got it, sorry." Anna folded her hands in her lap, thankful she had found her mittens before she ran out of the house. She was only trying to make conversation. How could she know Kristoff didn't live in a house like she did? And here she was running away from her home without permission to try to save Arendelle. Her parents would understand—she hoped.

Although they might not be thrilled when they learned she had left Harmon with the ice deliverer, who was practically a total stranger.

What was she thinking?

How was a girl who had never left her village before going to save the entire kingdom from a freak summer snowstorm?

By following her heart, she decided. Call it intuition or her gut, but she knew someone was out there looking for her. Either that, or the snow was making her a little batty already.

The sled hit a bump and she bumped into Kristoff. She locked eyes with him for a moment, her cheeks burning before they both looked away. Anna slid over so that it wouldn't happen again.

"Hang on," he said, staring straight ahead as he cracked the reins. "We like to go fast."

Fast was exactly what she needed. She had to get to Arendelle, figure out where this weather was coming from, and get back to Harmon before her parents started to worry. Who was she kidding? They were probably already worried.

Relax, Anna, she told herself. *Focus on your plan, and try to enjoy the ride.* She was finally leaving the village! She put her feet up on the front of Kristoff's sleigh. "I like fast."

"Whoa, whoa, whoa!" Kristoff nudged her boots. "Get your feet down. This is fresh lacquer. Seriously, were you raised in a barn?" He spit on the wood and wiped the area where her feet had been. His spittle went flying into her eye.

Anna wiped her face with the back of her mitten. "No, I was raised in a bakery. What about you?"

"I was raised not far from here." He kept his eyes on the path. "Stay alert. We need to watch for wolves."

Anna sighed. He wasn't going to reveal anything about himself, was he?

She really was traveling to Arendelle with a total stranger.

Well, he couldn't stay a stranger for long. Not when they had a two-day journey ahead of them to get down the mountain to Arendelle.

When they got tired, they made camp in someone's barn. Kristoff didn't even ask if they could use it ("Who's coming out to check on us in this weather?"). Then they rose before the sun to journey on. Anna watched as

Arendelle grew closer and closer. As the castle came into view that afternoon, she was too in awe to talk anymore. Arendelle was just like she pictured it in her mind. Even covered in snow and ice, the castle was magnificent nestled among the mountains. And the village surrounding it was ten times the size of Harmon.

"Whoa, look at the fjord," Kristoff said, pointing to the harbor.

Dozens of ships listed on the frozen water. Covered in snow and ice, they looked like a ship graveyard. The village was equally eerie. Even though it was the middle of the afternoon, no one was outside in this weather. Everywhere, lanterns and green-and-gold flags bearing Princess Elsa's silhouette were frozen solid.

"We should find the castle courtyard," Kristoff suggested. "Maybe someone there will know what's going on."

"Make a right at the butcher's shop next to the stables," Anna said without thinking.

Kristoff did a double take. "I thought you'd never been here before."

The butcher's shop was straight ahead. The stables were next to it, but she was certain the courtyard was around the corner. Anna felt a tingle go up her spine. "I haven't." How did she know where to go?

Kristoff followed Anna's directions to the castle courtyard.

A crowd was gathered around a large bonfire burning near the castle gates. He dismounted and gave Sven carrots.

"Let's see what's going on," Anna suggested, and patted Sven on the back. "Nice job, buddy. Why don't you take a rest for a bit?" Sven looked happy to oblige.

As they got closer, Anna could see men in green uniforms passing out blankets and cloaks to villagers waiting in line. Someone was also directing them to where they could get a mug of hot glogg. Anna looked up and gasped. The water in the fountain had frozen midstream, curving in a pattern that was both beautiful and frightening. She'd never seen water freeze like that before. In the middle of the fountain stood a bronze sculpture of the king, the queen, and the princess as a young girl. Anna leaned on the fountain railing, trying to get a closer look. Then she heard someone shouting.

"The future queen has cursed this land!"

A small, skinny man with glasses, a white mustache, and a military uniform was standing on the castle steps, talking to anyone who would listen.

Future queen? Cursed? There was that word again. Anna joined a group of people standing in front of him.

"Why would she want to hurt Arendelle?" someone asked, and others murmured in agreement.

"She wouldn't!" another man interrupted. He was

dark-haired and large around the middle, and his face seemed kind, unlike the little man's. "My dear people, your future queen would never hurt you. We are doing everything we can to find the princess and stop this winter. As I've been saying for the past few days, the castle is open to anyone who needs it. We have enough food and blankets for everyone."

"Don't be a fool!" the short man snapped. "Food will eventually run out. We cannot survive in this strange weather forever!"

"Don't listen to the Duke of Weselton," Lord Peterssen countered. "We must stay calm."

"What are we going to do?" asked a woman with a baby bundled up inside her cloak. "All of my vegetables have died in this weather!"

"We weren't prepared for winter in the middle of the summer," a man shouted. "We haven't even begun to hunt for food for the cold season. There won't be enough to eat this winter if the weather doesn't change soon."

The Duke smiled. "Do not fear! Prince Hans of the Southern Isles will save us all."

The crowd clapped half-heartedly, but Lord Peterssen mumbled something and turned away. Anna was glad to hear this Prince Hans was supposedly going to save them, but how? And from what? Could he change the weather?

"Excuse me, but who is Prince Hans?" she spoke up.

"What are you doing?" Kristoff muttered fiercely under his breath.

"Getting answers." Anna grabbed his hand and dragged him with her, snaking through the crowd until they were standing right in front of the castle steps.

"Weren't you listening?" the Duke asked rudely. "The prince has been staying in Arendelle for a while and is well versed in matters of the kingdom. He has graciously agreed to step in and fix this situation. We must stop her before we're too late."

"Stop who?" Anna asked.

The Duke rolled back his shoulders. "Did you not see for yourself what she did? With such a large crowd gathered for the coronation? She nearly killed me!"

"No, I'm sorry, I didn't see anything," Anna said. "We just journeyed down the mountain. My village is way up there." She pointed to a tiny speck that was almost completely obscured. "We were preparing to celebrate the queen's coronation when this unusual weather blew in. We're worried about what's happening, too, which is why we're here for answers. So I apologize, but who are you talking about?"

"The princess!" The Duke jumped up and down like a toddler. "She's a monster!"

"The princess?" Anna repeated, her heart thumping

wildly as a ringing started in her ears. *I have to find her,* she thought suddenly, but she wasn't sure why she thought she could. "Why would Princess Elsa try to hurt you?"

"She didn't," interrupted Lord Peterssen. "The princess wouldn't hurt anyone. She was frightened and ran off, but she'll return. She'd never abandon her people." He glared at the Duke. "And I would prefer if you didn't call the future queen a monster."

"She froze the fjord!" a man called out. "We can't get our ships in or out of the harbor!"

"We're trapped here because of her!" someone else yelled.

"How am I going to feed my family if we can't get food?" a woman cried while a baby wailed in the distance. "Her magic has frozen the whole kingdom. If it is no better where these people have come from, we are truly doomed!"

"Wait," Kristoff interrupted. "Are you telling me the future queen caused this snowstorm? How?"

"Sorcery! Witchcraft!" the Duke railed. "After her powers were revealed, she fled across the fjord, creating this eternal winter. She must be stopped! Prince Hans went after the princess. He is hoping to talk some sense into her."

"The princess has powers?" Anna asked. "She made all this snow and ice? Why, that's incredible!"

The Duke narrowed his eyes at her. "Who are you, girl?"

Kristoff stood taller, shifting his body slightly in front of hers. She nudged him aside.

"Someone who wants to stop this winter as much as you do," Anna said firmly. "And I don't see how threatening the princess will help anyone."

The Duke was grim. "I suggest you find somewhere to keep warm until Prince Hans returns. You'll never make it back up the mountain in these conditions. It's growing colder. This winter won't end till we find the princess and make her stop the madness." He headed back into the castle, and the crowd started to disperse.

"Wait!" Anna cried. The Duke ignored her. There was something about that man she did not like. "You expect this Prince Hans to find her on his own?" Anna ran after them. No one was listening. "Wait!" She turned back to Kristoff. He and Lord Peterssen were the only people still standing there. "If the princess caused this winter, it had to be by mistake. She must feel so helpless!"

Lord Peterssen rubbed his hands in front of the fire to keep warm. "And frightened. I imagine she kept these powers from all of us for fear of how we'd react—and people are as frightened as she feared. Maybe if she just came back and explained herself . . ." He looked up at the sky as snowflakes fell on his face. "I just hope we find her before it's too late."

Anna stared again at the bronze statue of the royal family covered in ice. "Her magic and what she's capable of is so beautiful."

"*If* one is prepared for this kind of weather," Kristoff said, standing close to the fire. "No one wants to see snow in the middle of the summer."

"No, they do not." Lord Peterssen rubbed his hands to keep warm. "I just hope Prince Hans finds her and convinces her to come back to us so we can fix this."

"Do you have any idea where she went?" Anna asked.

"I didn't see the princess run," Lord Peterssen admitted, "but many saw her flee across the fjord and head in the direction of the North Mountain. It isn't much to go on, I know." He rubbed his arms. "If you'll excuse me, I'm going back inside. Please have some hot glogg before you journey home again. Hopefully this weather will turn before you must go back."

"Go back? But . . ." She couldn't go back yet. Now that she knew the storm was caused by magic, she couldn't just walk away. She had to help bring back summer and find the princess.

Anna understood why the princess would be frightened, but why head to the North Mountain? Was something up there? Her skin prickled. *I think I'm supposed to help her.* The closer she got to the castle, the more she felt it. Now her gut was telling her to walk into the castle, but that didn't make sense. If the people were right, Elsa was halfway up the North Mountain. Still, staring up at the lit windows and archways of the castle, Anna felt a magnetic pull. She knew something was waiting for her inside.

"Do you want some glogg?" Kristoff asked, pulling her from her thoughts. "I've never been a fan, but if we're going to begin the journey back to Harmon to tell everyone what's going on, then we should probably eat and drink something. And get more carrots for Sven." He watched Anna walk right past him. "Hey! Where are you going?"

Anna climbed the castle steps to the entrance. There were no guards to be seen, and the crowd had dispersed. If there was ever a good moment to enter, this was it.

"Hey, hey, hey!" Kristoff rushed in front of her. "You can't just walk inside the royal castle uninvited!"

"I am invited! Sort of. Didn't Lord Peterssen say the castle was open if anyone needed it?" Anna ducked under his arm and continued up the stairs. The coast was still clear. She could make it inside unnoticed and then . . . well, who knew? She just had to get inside.

"Lord Peterssen meant if you needed help." Kristoff slid on a patch of ice on the steps. "The glogg is outside the entrance. He didn't mean go inside."

But she had to get inside. It was as if the place were

calling to her. She could feel it in her bones, but she didn't know how to explain that to Kristoff. "No one is even guarding the entrance. It's like someone *wants* us to come in. I'll only be a minute. I just need to see something."

"Anna!" Kristoff tried to keep up with her.

She reached the top step and opened the door. The second she walked inside, she felt a strange calm come over her. Anna stared up at the high vaulted ceiling in the two-story entranceway. The room had a central staircase with two sets of stairs that both led to a second-story landing. Portraits decorated the walls on both levels. *Why does this room seem so familiar?* she wondered. *I've never been here before.* She glanced up at the central staircase again and had a sudden vision of a redheaded girl in a nightgown and bare feet racing down the staircase, giggling.

Anna jumped in surprise. "It's me," she said softly, running toward the stairs.

"Don't go upstairs! Are you crazy?" Kristoff grabbed her arm but stopped talking when he saw her expression. "What is it?"

The image vanished. *This doesn't make sense.* Anna's knees buckled.

"Whoa!" Kristoff held her up. "What's going on?"

"I thought . . . I . . ." Anna wasn't sure how to explain what she had just seen without sounding crazy. She spun around, trying to get her bearings, and spotted the portrait of the royal family. Anna stepped closer, staring at the picture curiously. *Freya?* Anna gasped in surprise. The queen and Freya looked exactly alike. *How is that possible?* she thought, and reached up to touch the painting then saw a flash. She saw her younger self sitting on a bench with her legs dangling while someone painted her portrait. "Anna, hold still!" the person said. She felt her knees wobble again.

"Are you okay?" Kristoff asked.

"It's so strange, but I feel like I've been here before." Anna clung to his arm so she wouldn't fall.

"Have you?" Kristoff asked quietly.

Anna looked at him. Her voice was small. "No."

"We should leave," he said, sounding worried.

Anna shook her head. "We can't. There's something here I'm meant to find." She let go of him and headed up the staircase to the next floor. This time he didn't stop her. Kristoff silently followed her down the long hallway past several rooms. She heard the wind howling outside the windows as she climbed another staircase. She stopped abruptly when she saw a wall of jagged icicles blocking their path.

Kristoff touched the sharp point on one of the icicles. "What happened here?"

"It had to be the princess when she was trying to get away," Anna guessed. But what had frightened her in the first place? The ice she'd created looked almost like a sculpture, twisting and turning into a shape Anna couldn't put her finger on. She'd never seen anything like it before. "I never knew winter could be so magical."

"Yeah . . . it really is beautiful, isn't it?" someone behind them said. "But it's so colorless. You know, how about a little variety? Must we bleach the joy out of it all?"

Anna and Kristoff turned around and immediately jumped. The person speaking was a walking, talking snowman with short, stout legs, a plump bottom, a thin oval head, teeth, and a carrot nose. A cloud with a flurry followed him.

"I'm thinking like maybe some crimson, chartreuse . . ." The snowman continued to babble as he approached. "How 'bout yellow? No, not yellow. Yellow and snow? Brrr . . . no go. Am I right?" He blinked at Anna.

Anna screamed and reflexively kicked his head, sending it flying off his body and into Kristoff's arms.

"Hi!" the head said.

"You're creepy!" Kristoff tossed the snowman's head back to Anna.

"I don't want it!" Anna threw it back to him.

"Back atcha!" Kristoff sent it her way again.

"Please don't drop me," the head said as its body ran at her, waving its twig arms.

Now Anna felt bad. "Sorry. I won't." She was talking to a snowman. How was that possible?

"All right," the head said. "We got off to a bad start. Can you put me back together?" The body waited patiently next to her.

Was the snowman serious? Carefully, she reached out with the head. "Ew! Ew!" Anna cried as she placed it back onto his body. In her haste, she put the head on upside down.

The snowman looked confused. "Wait, what am I looking at right now? Why are you hanging from the ceiling like a bat?"

Anna knelt down. "Okay, wait a second." She flipped his head the right way.

"Ooh! Thank you!" the snowman said. "Now everything's perfect!"

Anna wasn't sure about perfect. It was snowing in the middle of the summer, the princess had the power to create ice, they were talking to a snowman, and Anna was having the strangest sense of déjà vu standing in the middle of Arendelle Castle. She stared harder at the snowman. He seemed familiar as well, from the curve of his head to his front teeth and twig hair. *He's the snowman from my dreams!* she realized. *He inspired my cookies. How can that be if I'm just meeting him for the first time?* She started to hyperventilate. Kristoff stared at her strangely.

"I didn't mean to scare you! Let's start over," the snowman told her. "Hi, everyone. I'm Olaf, and I like warm hugs."

She tried to calm herself down. "Olaf," Anna repeated. *I know this name. Why?*

"And you are . . . ?" Olaf looked at her patiently.

"Oh . . . um, I'm Anna."

"Anna? Huh." Olaf scratched his chin. "I think I was supposed to remember something about an Anna. I'm not sure what it was, though."

Anna's heart started to beat fast again. She moved in closer. "You were?"

"And you are . . . ?" Olaf asked Kristoff as he pulled off one of the snowman's twig arms.

"Fascinating," Kristoff muttered as the twig arm he was holding continued to move even though it wasn't attached to Olaf's body.

"He's Kristoff," Anna replied. "We came here together." She watched the snowman continue to move around. If Elsa could make ice, then maybe she could make a walking, talking snowman, too. "Olaf . . . did Elsa build you?"

"Yeah. Why?" Olaf replied.

Progress!

"Do you know where she is?" Anna held her breath.

"Yeah. Why?" Olaf asked again.

Her palms began to sweat. This felt right. She was on to something. Olaf knew where to find the princess. "Do you think you could show us the way?"

Kristoff bent the twig. Instead of snapping, it bent right back into place. "How does this thing work?" he interrupted. The twig smacked Kristoff in the face.

"Hey!" Olaf snatched the arm back and stuck it onto his body. "Trying to concentrate here." He looked at Anna again. "Yeah. Why?"

"I'll tell you why. We need Elsa to bring back summer," Kristoff said.

"Summer!" Olaf gasped. "Oh, I don't know why, but I've always loved summer, and sun, and all things hot."

"Really?" Kristoff almost laughed. "I'm guessing you don't have much experience with heat."

"Of course I do," Olaf argued. "I've lived through winter, spring, summer, and fall, but I've always seen it through Elsa's window." He sighed. "Sometimes I like to close my eyes and imagine what it would be like to experience weather outside the castle. Or even outside Elsa's chambers, but I guess I'm doing that now. I couldn't wait anymore. Elsa didn't come back after Hans and the Duke came for her, so I wanted to go find her." He looked at Anna. "She was looking for you."

"Me?" Anna stepped back, bumping into Kristoff. "She doesn't even know me." Her heart was beating so fast it felt like it would come out of her chest. In her head, images flashed by again. She heard the little girl she had seen on the stairs laughing and saw, again, the image of herself on a bench while someone drew her. Neither of those things had happened before. She'd never been to Arendelle or the castle, yet it, too, seemed familiar. And now finding Olaf—that felt like it was meant to be. She wasn't sure why Olaf thought he knew her, but her heart said he might be right.

"Are you sure about that?" Olaf asked.

"Olaf? Will you help us find Elsa?" She held out her hand. Olaf took it and toddled down the hall, heading for the stairs. "Come on! Elsa's this way. Let's go bring back summer!"

Kristoff shook his head as he followed. "Are we really listening to a talking snowman now?"

Anna looked back at him. "Yes! We can't go back to Harmon yet. Not if we can help find the princess and stop this winter."

Kristoff sighed. "Fine, but Sven isn't going to like this."

Anna gave the castle one last lingering look. She had a feeling she'd be back. She wasn't sure what her purpose was yet, but something told her finding Elsa would give her the answers she needed.

She was so preoccupied she didn't notice the Duke standing in the shadows, watching the unlikely trio leave the castle.

CHAPTER TWENTY

Elsa

As Elsa set off on her new journey, she realized she had no idea how to find the Valley of the Living Rock. In her memory, she hadn't looked at landmarks or paid attention to the route her family took. She was just a child. And now, with the kingdom covered in white, it made finding her way even harder. What she really needed was a map. But would a regular map mark off a magical location such as the valley?

There was only one way to find out. She needed to locate someone who lived in the mountains and might know the area. Elsa used her magic to quicken her search, creating a sleigh made out of ice to take her down the mountain. The sleigh gained speed as she crossed into the forest. When she saw a smokestack in the distance, she headed directly for it.

The building was partially covered in a snowdrift. Ice had frozen on the sign on the porch. Elsa tapped it and the ice broke off, allowing her to read the sign: Wandering Oaken's Trading Post and Sauna. Elsa paused before knocking. What if someone inside recognized her? Walking into the shop wearing an evening gown would give her away. With a wave of her hand, Elsa created a sparkling royal blue hooded cloak. She pulled the hood over her head and hoped it hid her familiar face. Then she walked up the steps and into the shop.

A man in a patterned sweater with a matching hat was seated behind a counter. "Hoo-hoo! Big summer blowout!" he said. "Half off swimming suits, clogs, and a sun balm of my own invention. If you're looking for cold weather gear, we don't have much left in our winter department." He pointed to a sparse corner of the shop that had a lone snowshoe sitting in it.

"Thank you, but I have all I need for this weather." Elsa stood in the shadows as she looked around the dimly lit space. The shelves were cramped with supplies from ice axes to clothing and food. "What I really need is a map." She paused. "Or directions to the Valley of the Living Rock."

His blue eyes widened. "Ooh, yes, a map I have, *ja*? But I don't know of this place you mention, dear." He shimmied out from behind the narrow counter, trying hard to keep his large frame from knocking over any of the books stacked on the shelf behind him. He unfurled a large scroll and showed it to Elsa, pointing out different landmarks. One looked like a rocky area just northwest of where Elsa's sleigh was stopped. "I hope you find what you're looking for, even if this isn't the weather to be traveling in. The only one crazy enough to be out in this storm is you, dear," Oaken added. "A real howler in July, huh? Wherever could it be coming from?"

"The North Mountain," she murmured without thinking. She pressed some coins into Oaken's hand. "Thank you for the map." She shuffled out again and discarded her cloak.

Oaken had been right about the howler part: the wind had picked up that day, and many areas were now covered in a thick ice. Elsa climbed into her sleigh again and, using her magic to propel her, crossed the river and glided along while watching closely for the rocky area that she suspected could be the valley. Slowly the landscape started to change. Snow-covered trees gave way to large boulders. Something about it looked familiar. Elsa stopped and hid the sleigh behind a row of trees, then followed a craggy path until she reached what seemed to be an entrance to the valley. As she as she got closer, she knew she was in the right place. The valley looked just like it had in her memories;

steam-billowing geysers dotted the wide-open spaces of the landscape, which was seemingly untouched by the deep freeze over the kingdom. A low-lying fog made it difficult to see, but she recognized a circle where hundreds of small boulders sat in a strange formation. As she neared them, her breath hastened. These were the boulders in her vision that had rocked and rolled when her father called to the trolls.

"Hello?" Elsa heard her voice echo from the walls of the mountains. "I need your help." The rocks didn't move, so she tried a different approach. "Grand Pabbie? It is Princess Elsa of Arendelle. I am trying to find my sister."

Suddenly, the boulders began to shake. Elsa stepped back as they tumbled toward her, a large one rolling to a stop at her feet and transforming into a troll. The other boulders became trolls as well. She knew immediately that the one with the yellow crystal necklace and mossy robe was the one she was looking for.

"Grand Pabbie?" she asked, and he nodded. "I am here to seek your help."

"Princess Elsa," he said in a gravelly voice. "It has been a long time."

Elsa glanced at the whites of his big eyes. "I'm looking for my sister. The kingdom doesn't seem to know of her existence, but I remember her. The memories came flooding back the morning of my coronation when I saw a portrait of my parents and me with a small redheaded girl. I knew immediately it was Anna."

Grand Pabbie nodded. "I see."

"My parents brought Anna and me to you for help when we were children." Tears started to flow before she could stop them. "I know I accidentally struck her with my magic, but I didn't mean to hurt her," she whispered.

"Of course not, child." Grand Pabbie reached out, and Elsa knelt down in front of him and put her hands in his. His were coarse and cold.

"I didn't want her to forget my magic, but somehow in interfering with your spell, I must have messed up everything," she said, getting choked up. "I lost my sister and my powers in the process."

"It was a grave mistake," he agreed.

"I didn't learn I still had powers until a few years ago. They suddenly reappeared when my parents died," Elsa added. The memory was still so painful that it hurt to talk about.

"We were all sorry to hear of your parents' passing," Grand Pabbie said, and the trolls around him nodded.

"Thank you. Life without them has been difficult," Elsa admitted. "Learning I have a sister has given me hope again." Tears sprang to her eyes. "Now I can think of nothing else but finding her. Can you help me?"

"Elsa, I feel your pain, but you must listen to me," Grand Pabbie said, and a hush fell over the other trolls. "You cannot try to find her."

Elsa pulled her hands away. "Why not?"

"The curse that has kept you apart is something even I cannot fully understand," he explained. "If you remember Anna, then that magic is starting to fade, but until this curse holding you both is broken, you cannot intervene."

Curse? Intervene? All she wanted was to see her sister. "I don't understand." Elsa started to cry in earnest. "How are we cursed? You truly won't help me find her? Anna is the only family I have left."

Grand Pabbie sighed deeply. "It's not that I won't. I can't. You just need to hold on a little while longer."

"Hold on? We've been separated for years!" She was sobbing now. "Anna is all I have left. Why would you use magic to keep us apart?"

"You have been through so much, child, I know. What is the last thing you remember?" he asked.

"The last thing I saw in my vision was me reaching out to stop you from erasing Anna's memories." Elsa looked at him. "I feared my magic had killed her, but then I found a letter from my parents that explained Anna was alive. But . . . I had to leave before I could find out where she was and why we were separated."

He held out his hands again. "Perhaps I can fill in the rest." He touched his forehead, then swept his hand into the air. A bluish-white line of stars followed his fingers, sweeping into the sky, where an image from the past appeared that both Elsa and the trolls could see. Elsa recognized the image immediately: it showed her parents, and Anna, and herself, on the night she accidentally struck her sister with her magic.

The memory replayed the vision she had seen on her coronation day, and once again she saw her much younger self reach out to keep Grand Pabbie from erasing Anna's memories. Grand Pabbie and her mother tried to stop her, but they had been too late. Once her hand connected with the troll's, there was an explosion of blue light. That was where Elsa's memory had ended, but Grand Pabbie's vision kept going.

Elsa watched as her younger self and Grand Pabbie were thrown backward. Trolls ran for cover as Papa shielded Mama and Anna. When the dust cleared, she saw her younger self unconscious on the ground. Mama gently put Anna down and ran to Elsa's side.

"What happened to my daughter?" Papa rushed over. The image was almost too much to bear.

"My powers connected with Elsa's." Grand Pabbie was out of breath. "I believe it changed the magic somehow."

"What does that mean?" Papa asked.

To Elsa's horror, while they spoke, Anna slowly began to freeze from the tips of her shoes up to her legs. In seconds, ice would overtake Anna's whole body.

Grand Pabbie turned around just in time. "Your Majesty, grab Elsa!" he called to the king. "Run to higher ground! Quickly!"

Papa scooped up Elsa in his arms and ran up the stone steps to the entrance of the valley. When Mama saw Anna's small body slowly turning to ice she ran for her, but could do nothing to stop it. Neither could Grand Pabbie. Elsa felt her heart beat wildly as she watched the scene. It was pandemonium. Even some of the trolls were crying out and frightened. But as the distance between Anna's and Elsa's bodies increased, the ice on Anna began to melt. Mama picked Anna up and held her close, crying softly in relief.

"What just happened to Anna?" Mama cried. "I don't understand. I thought you removed the ice."

Grand Pabbie knelt down by Anna's side and placed his hands on her head. He looked from Anna to the king, who held Elsa on higher ground. Everyone watched as Grand Pabbie made his way up to the king and placed his hands on Elsa's head as well. The valley was quiet as he came back down to the center of the circle to the queen.

"Grand Pabbie, what is it?" one of the trolls asked.

"I'm afraid they've been cursed," Grand Pabbie whispered.

"Cursed?" Mama repeated. "How?"

"It happened when Elsa's and my magic crossed," he explained. "We were both trying to accomplish different things with magic—I wanted to remove Anna's memories of magic, while Elsa wanted to keep them. The combination caused something else to happen entirely—a curse." He looked back and forth between the king and the queen. "It appears Elsa has forgotten her powers."

"But she will remember them, right?" Mama asked.

"Eventually. For now, her powers are wrapped up in her fear for her sister," Grand Pabbie explained. "She won't remember how to use them till this strange magic fades."

"And when will that be?" Papa asked.

Grand Pabbie's face was solemn. "When she needs her sister more than she ever has before."

"But they need each other now," Mama said, the desperation in her voice clear.

"We don't always get what we want—that's what curses teach us," Grand Pabbie told her gently. "Magic can be unpredictable, especially when more than one kind interacts. It appears the curse affected each sister differently. Anna cannot be near Elsa without ice consuming her body and traveling to her heart. If it stays there too long, it grows, as ice can do, and it will eventually kill her." Mama burst into tears. "And Elsa, while physically fine, cannot survive long-term if she is missing the love of her sister. She is her greatest joy."

Elsa watched Grand Pabbie's memory in agony. This was all her fault. If she hadn't tried to stop Grand Pabbie's spell, Anna wouldn't have been hurt. This was why they had been separated: Elsa's being near Anna could kill her. How had Elsa's parents ever forgiven her for what she had done?

"Can you reverse the spell?" Papa asked hoarsely.

Grand Pabbie looked to the sky, then down at the earth before he spoke. "I don't believe that's possible." Mama cried harder. "But there is hope. Magic wrapped up in emotions like Elsa's fades over time. This curse won't last forever. When the time is right—and the girls need each other more than ever before—their curse will be broken."

The queen looked up with bloodshot eyes. "You mean someday it will be safe for Anna and Elsa to be together?"

"Yes." Grand Pabbie looked up at the aurora borealis that shone above them. "I know this isn't the answer you seek, but your daughters' love for each other can overcome any curse." Mama smiled through her tears. "For now, though, they must be kept apart. No one can say how long this magic will hold."

Throughout the grassy area, trolls whispered to one

another about the situation. Mama and Papa were trying to process their new reality, but it was clearly devastating.

"How will we explain this to them?" Mama asked. "They'll be heartbroken."

"The girls are always together," Papa told Grand Pabbie. "They won't want to be separated." He looked at Mama. "Can you imagine trying to keep them in separate wings of the castle?"

"No," Mama agreed. "Nor would it be safe. They wouldn't understand the consequences of being near one another. An accident could happen in a heartbeat. Putting this sort of responsibility on them at such a young age is impossible."

"This is true," Papa agreed. "And if word got out about what could happen to Anna if she was near Elsa, our enemies could try to use the knowledge to their advantage. We can't let our daughters be pawns in someone else's game," he said firmly.

"No." Tears streamed down Mama's cheeks. "What do we do?"

Grand Pabbie looked from Papa to Mama sadly. "Separate wings, I fear, are not enough. And the king is right—the world cannot know Anna and Elsa's weaknesses. They are both heirs to this kingdom. It's too dangerous."

Elsa could tell what Grand Pabbie was saying weighed heavily on her parents.

"They won't be able to stand the separation," Mama said. "I know my daughters."

Grand Pabbie thought for a moment. "Perhaps I can help." He looked at Mama. "Magic can still make the impossible possible. I could do a spell that will hide one of the children's identities from all but the two of you until the curse has lifted. It will keep both your daughters safe from harm in the kingdom, but it will also protect their fragile hearts if we remove their memories of each other as well." Mama looked startled. "Only until the curse lifts," he assured her. "If we do that, neither child will remember the other when they wake."

Realization of what the troll was saying was written all over Mama's face. She looked from one daughter to the other one, just feet away. "This feels so cruel. And yet, I don't believe we have any other choice." She looked at Papa. "At least they won't have to live with the truth their father and I possess."

Grand Pabbie looked at her sadly. "It is not fair," he agreed.

Mama rose to her full height. Her lower lip wobbled as she looked at Papa, her eyes filled with tears. "We have to let Grand Pabbie help them forget each other's existence until the curse lifts. We need to find someplace safe for one of them to go. It's the only way."

Papa appeared as devastated as Mama. "But how do we decide who stays with us?"

Even some of the trolls were weeping for the king and queen. Elsa watched the scene with tears streaming down her face. She felt her parents' pain. Mama finally spoke.

"Elsa will stay with us," she decided. "She is next in line to the throne, and her powers are too strong for her to control on her own." Papa was crying now, too. "You know this is how it has to be, Agnarr. Once Elsa remembers she has them, we need to be there to help her understand."

Papa nodded. "You are right. But where will Anna go?" His voice was breaking.

"Is there someone you trust to look after your daughter as if she were their own?" Grand Pabbie asked Mama.

"There is," she whispered. "I'd trust this friend with my life. But raising my daughter is a lot to ask."

"Nothing is too much to ask when it is done out of love," Grand Pabbie reminded her. "And to ease your anguish, Anna can be hidden in plain sight." Grand Pabbie looked at Mama. "You are the only two who will remember her true birthright. You can still see her when you want, but she won't know her true identity."

Papa and Mama looked at each other from across the valley. Both of them had tears steaming down their face. Papa turned to Grand Pabbie. "Do what you must. Just protect both our daughters." He hesitated, the words almost too hard for him to say out loud. "Help Elsa forget she has a sister, erase Anna's memories of her past life, and . . . remove Anna's existence from the kingdom's memory."

Watching them, Elsa understood her parents' decision, but she could also feel their pain, which mirrored her own. If only she hadn't interfered . . .

Closing his eyes, Grand Pabbie raised his hands to the stars again. The images of Anna's and Elsa's separate lives swept past them like clouds. He rolled the images into one and pressed a hand to Anna's forehead. Then he walked up the steps and did the same thing to Elsa. A flash of bright white light rippled across the valley like an earthquake, traveling to the far reaches of the kingdom before disappearing.

"It is done," Grand Pabbie said. "And now I have a gift—your future."

Grand Pabbie raised his hands into the sky again and showed Mama and Papa new images. One was of Anna playing happily in a village courtyard with a group of children. The other was of Elsa studying with her father in the library. Both girls were smiling. Both were thriving. They just weren't together. Mama and Papa attempted to smile through the sadness.

"When the time is right, they will remember and be reunited," Grand Pabbie promised.

That was the last thing Elsa heard before Grand Pabbie touched the memory in the sky and it seemingly swirled back into his hand, which he pressed again to his forehead. "Do you understand now why it isn't safe for you to find Anna?" he asked gently.

"But I remember Anna," Elsa said, her voice rising. "Doesn't that mean the curse is broken?"

Grand Pabbie shook his head. "It is starting to break, but if the curse were truly broken, not only would you remember your sister, the whole kingdom would as well."

Elsa's heart sank. Grand Pabbie was right. She was still the only one who knew who Anna was. Aside from Olaf, and he was an unreliable source at best. She tried to hold back fresh tears. "How do you know Anna doesn't remember me yet? What if she's out there right now looking for me, too?"

Grand Pabbie squeezed her hands. "I would know. You would, too. Elsa, you must stay calm—I can see beyond the valley, and I know what fear is doing to your magic. The kingdom is wrapped in an eternal winter."

"I didn't mean for that to happen," Elsa said softly. "I don't know how to fix it."

"You will figure it out," he assured her. "You must concentrate on controlling your powers. The rest will come. The magic is fading. I can feel it! You are remembering your past. Soon Anna will as well. But until she does, you must keep your distance. Your sister's life depends on it."

Elsa looked at the way out of the valley. Beyond the rocks, she saw the snow squall.

She had thought finding Anna would change everything, but she was wrong. Elsa had given her all the past few days and fought to find her family. She couldn't even do that now. If she got too close to Anna, ice would consume her.

Even after all that time, she was destined to be alone.

CHAPTER TWENTY-ONE

Anna

"Snow. Why did it have to be snow?" Anna asked, shivering as Kristoff and Sven led the sleigh into the mountains with her and Olaf tucked inside. "She couldn't have had tropical magic that covered the fjords in white sand and warm sunshine?"

"I love the sun!" Olaf butted in, his personal flurry crashing into the front seat of the sleigh as they bounced along the uneven path. "I mean, I think I like it. It's hard to tell what it does from inside the castle."

"I don't think you'd like it much." Kristoff squinted hard at the path ahead of them.

The snow had started to fall harder since they'd left Arendelle, and it was coming down in sheets. Anna wasn't sure how Kristoff and Sven could see where they were going.

Night had fallen, and the tiny lantern that hung off the edge of the sleigh wasn't giving much light. They'd have to find shelter somewhere soon, but Anna hadn't seen any houses or villages in hours. Suddenly, they came to a wall of snow that made the route impassable. The alternative was a hilly incline that didn't even look like a real path.

"Are you sure Elsa went this way?" Kristoff asked Olaf as he led Sven up the uncharted terrain that was covered in ice.

"Yes. No." Olaf scratched his head with one of his twigs. "Again, everything I saw was through a window. I heard shouting and saw ice freezing, and then I looked out and saw Elsa—at least, I think it was Elsa, because who else can make snow?—running across the fjord as it turned to ice. Then she disappeared into the trees!" Olaf frowned. "And I lost sight of her."

Kristoff took his eyes off the path and looked at Anna. "Remind me again why we listened to a talking snowman? We're in deep snow, the wind is howling, we have no shelter, and I'm sledding up a mountain based on a hunch."

"It's not like we had a better option," Anna pointed out. "It's going to be fine! Olaf will help us find her. He knows Elsa better than anyone, don't you?"

"Yes!" Olaf insisted as the sleigh took a narrow turn and

started to climb again. "I know lots about Elsa, because she made me three years ago and I never left her room." His eyes lit up. "Wait! I'm wrong. Sometimes she snuck me through one of the secret passageways and we went up to the bell tower or the attic. Once, we got to go to the Great Hall and Elsa made a giant snow hill that we slid down. But that was in the middle of the night."

Anna felt the hair on the back of her neck stand up. Suddenly she remembered being very small and sliding down a snow hill inside a giant hall with a blond girl—and they were both holding on to a snowman. She looked at Olaf again. "Did you just do that?"

"Do what?" Olaf asked.

"Make me see that," Anna answered. Maybe the cold was getting to her.

"See what?" Olaf asked as the sleigh hit a rock and took air. It crashed back down, and Olaf's flurry smacked Anna and Kristoff in the face.

Anna rubbed her eyes and felt the memory fading away.

The gruff look on Kristoff's face was replaced with an expression of mild concern. "I think you've been in the cold too long."

"I think so, too," Anna agreed. "I'm starting to see things that aren't there." She glanced at the snowman again. "Like you. At least, I think it was you. The two of us were riding a snow hill together inside a big room."

"That's because we did!" Olaf said.

Anna's breath started to come faster. "When?"

Her parents had told her they'd adopted her as a baby, but what if that wasn't true? Anna's earliest memories with Tomally and Johan were later—starting school, standing on a stool and baking bread next to her mother, waiting for Freya to pull up outside their home. In all those, she was a girl of about six or seven. True, no one remembered being a baby, but the little girl in her visions looked and sounded just like her. She couldn't be more than four or five. What were these sudden flashes of memories she couldn't fully remember? Were they memories of her first family?

Sometimes she wondered who her birth parents were and why they had given her up, but she never asked Tomally or Johan. She didn't want to hurt them by asking. She always said the only thing she remembered about her former life was being kissed by a troll. It had seemed a funny thing to say when other kids asked about her adoption, but the truth was—she really remembered this happening. It felt like a dream—a fuzzy memory, really— of being asleep while a troll talked to her and then kissed her on the forehead. She had seen it in her dreams so many times that she truly believed it. She just didn't share that with other people.

She'd mentioned it to her parents once or twice. Now that she thought about it, they'd never denied it.

"Olaf?" Anna tried again. "Did you and I really go sledding . . . indoors?" Olaf nodded. "But how is that possible? I'd never left my village before this trip. Are you sure you haven't traveled anywhere outside the castle?"

Olaf's face fell. "I don't think so. Have I?"

"I don't know," Anna said, feeling frustrated.

"Neither do I," Olaf admitted.

"Can you two stop talking?" Kristoff cracked the reins again. "It's getting harder and harder to see with all this snow. I'm trying to concentrate. This path is too rocky to stay on. We need to find you somewhere warm to thaw out and then figure out where we're going next. We are not staying on a wild-goose chase with a talking snowman who doesn't know where he's going."

"But—" Anna said.

Kristoff ignored her. "Give me a second." He stood up, holding the lantern into the growing darkness. "I thought we were near the valley, but all this snow is changing the view."

"Which valley?" Anna asked. She was suddenly shivering.

"A valley that has no snow," Kristoff said, sounding as if he'd answered without thinking.

"How can a valley have no snow when the whole kingdom is covered in snow?" Olaf asked.

"How can a snowman talk?" Kristoff countered.

In the distance, they heard a wolf howl.

I need to find Elsa, Anna realized, the need almost overwhelming her.

She closed her eyes, trying to shut out the strange thoughts. Maybe Kristoff was right: she needed sleep. "I don't feel right," she said, and leaned her head down on the sleigh.

"Anna?" Kristoff shook her. "Don't fall asleep. You hear me? We're going to find shelter." He sat her up. "Olaf, I can't believe I'm going to say this, but keep talking to her till I can find us somewhere to stop."

"Okay, about what?" Olaf asked.

"Maybe about why the princess went all ice crazy?" Kristoff snapped the reins again, and Sven continued to climb.

Anna gave him a dirty look. "She's not crazy, she's—" Another flash caused her head to feel like it was going to explode.

Elsa, do the magic! Do the magic! she heard a small voice say. Next she saw herself sitting on a chair in her nightgown, clapping her hands. Had she just said the name Elsa? That was impossible! Anna started to hyperventilate. *What is happening to me?*

"Faster, Sven!" Kristoff cried, holding Anna up with one hand. "Anna? Stay with me, okay? Hang on."

"Trying," Anna whispered, but her head felt like it was on fire and she was so tired.

"Talk to her, Olaf!" Kristoff shouted. "What can you tell us about Elsa?"

"She loved flowers. Hans sent her purple heather every week," Olaf told them. "He was one of the only people who could get her to leave her room."

"That's nice," Anna said dreamily.

Kristoff shook her again. "Olaf! Keep talking!"

"She loved gloves!" Olaf added, bouncing so high in his seat that his head popped off for a second. "She always wore blue ones, even in the summer, and I started to wonder . . . maybe she has a thing about dirt. Oh! And she liked to read maps and books the king and queen left her. I never met them," he said sadly. "Elsa told me that was when she stopped coming out of her room. Until this year, when she had to get ready to be queen. Then she had to leave her room a lot."

"That's so sad," Anna said. Her voice seemed far away. "It was like she was locking herself away from the world. Sometimes I felt like that in Harmon—kept apart from the rest of the kingdom. I wanted to see more."

"You will—but you have to stay awake. *Barn!*" Kristoff shouted. "Thank goodness. Stop, Sven!"

Anna saw the barn through the driving snow and then the world went dark.

———

Next thing she knew, she was somewhere warm and she could smell hay. She heard a fire crackling nearby. Her eyes fluttered open.

"There you are!" Kristoff said. "You've been out for hours. Olaf, she's awake! I thought . . . I don't know." He ran a hand through his hair. "You need . . . you need soup."

Sven snorted.

"Soup?" Anna said groggily. She was covered in a wool blanket and appeared to be in a large barn. She could see horses nibbling hay in their stalls and chickens in their coop. A cow mooed close by. Everyone was sheltered indoors in this weather.

"Yes, she needs soup," Kristoff argued with the reindeer. "She needs to eat something. She didn't have any glogg at the castle like I did, and you ate all the carrots." Sven snorted again. "I'm just concerned, that's all." Sven pawed at the ground. "Yes, that's *all*. Enough, Sven." Kristoff held out a mug. "Here. You'll be happy to know I asked the family if we could stay in the barn this time, and they said yes. They were just happy to get news from Arendelle. Not that we have much news, but seeing a talking snowman seemed to make the kids happy."

Olaf giggled. "They liked my personal flurry, but they said they were tired of the snow."

"Even I'm tired of the snow, and I harvest ice for a living," Kristoff said. "Anna? Have some soup."

She sat up slowly. Her head was still pounding. She groaned.

Kristoff held the mug to her lips. "Come on. Just have a little."

Anna took a sip, feeling the soup warm her insides. For someone who was so cranky all the time, Kristoff could be really sweet when he wanted to be. "Thank you."

Kristoff blushed. "Yeah, well . . ." Sven snorted again and Kristoff looked away. "You're welcome. I just need to get you home in one piece. And that's where we're going—home."

Anna's eyes widened. "We can't! We've got to find Elsa!"

Kristoff sat back and sighed. "Look at how sick you're getting in this weather."

"It's not the weather," Anna insisted, but she couldn't explain what she was feeling. She knew it sounded crazy, but something told her they needed to keep going until they found Elsa. Maybe Elsa would understand what was happening to her. After all, she knew magic. "Someone's got to convince her to bring back summer. She'll listen to Olaf, and if not, we'll make her listen to us."

"It's getting colder." Kristoff put down the mug of soup,

which Sven immediately started to lap up. "We can't keep riding around when Olaf has no clue where he's going. I know you want to help, but it's impossible when all we have to go on is a vague suggestion that she was headed toward the North Mountain. Let's face it: no one knows where Princess Elsa really is."

"The Valley of the Living Rock!" Olaf blurted out.

Kristoff's eyes widened. "What did you say?"

"I've never heard of it," Anna told them.

"Neither have I," Olaf admitted. "Well, I have heard of it. I heard a man say the name when he read Elsa's letter from her mother. There was something about the Valley of the Living Rock. I'm just not sure where that is."

"I know where the Valley of the Living Rock is," Kristoff said.

"So you'll take me?" Anna asked.

Kristoff ran a hand through is hair. "Do I have to?"

She squeezed his hand. "Please?"

The fire crackled and popped as Anna waited for an answer. Olaf leaned in closer. Sven snorted. All eyes were on Kristoff, who was staring at Anna's hand. Finally, he looked up. His brown eyes were fiery in the glow of the flames. She'd never noticed his freckles before.

"Okay," Kristoff said. "We leave in the morning, but you'd better bundle up."

Anna smiled. For once, she didn't argue.

CHAPTER TWENTY-TWO

Elsa

Elsa had no idea how long it had been since she left the valley to head back to the North Mountain. If she couldn't be with Anna, time no longer mattered. Grand Pabbie's words played in a loop in her head. *Be patient.* She'd been more than patient! She had spent the past three years mourning their parents—whom Anna might not even remember—and had been without a sister since she was a child. Hadn't they both lost enough? When would this curse break? She remembered Anna; she needed Anna. Wasn't that what Grand Pabbie had said was needed for the magic to dissolve? Why didn't Anna remember her past as well?

What if Anna never remembered?

If Anna didn't remember her, then she didn't want to go on. She would stay at the top of the mountain until the curse broke, and if it didn't, then she'd stay there forever. Her people needed a strong leader, not a queen who was overcome with grief. They'd be better off without her.

Elsa's sleigh came to a halt at the steps leading to her ice palace. When she got out, she no longer looked at her kingdom in wonder. She was lost in her own misery. Maybe that was why she missed the footsteps in the snow leading to her palace doors. It wasn't until she was inside that she realized she wasn't alone.

Elsa jumped in shock. "How did you find me?"

"It isn't hard when you know where to look." Hans put his hands up to keep her from running away. "I came alone." He was dressed in a heavy navy coat and gloves, a scarf wrapped around his neck. Both a sword and a crossbow hung from a sheath on his belt. His boots were covered in snow, and his cheeks and nose were bright pink. She could only imagine the journey he had taken to get up the mountain.

"How did you . . ." Her voice trailed off.

Hans took a step closer. "When you ran off like that, freezing the fjord, I knew you were trying to disappear," he said. "So I thought: where is the farthest place Elsa could go to escape? And I looked up and saw it: the North Mountain."

Maybe Hans knew her better than she'd thought.

His eyes crinkled with worry. "Are you all right?"

No, she wanted to say. *I have a sister. She's alive. I desperately want to find her, but a curse is keeping us apart.* But she didn't.

Hans looked around in wonder. "You built this?"

"Yes," Elsa said, feeling humbled again by her creation. This wasn't some little igloo she had imagined. It had the architecture of her family castle, with snowflake designs and intricate patterns covering every wall and archway. Every pillar sparkled and glowed with a blue hue that bathed the whole palace in light.

"This place is incredible, and so are you," Hans said. "Everything about you feels different somehow."

She blushed. "Hans . . ."

"Is it your hair? You don't usually wear it down. I like your dress, too. This place suits you." Hans's eyes flickered to the room behind her. "You're here alone?"

She exhaled slowly. "I'm always alone."

Hans moved closer. "You're not alone, Elsa. I'm here for you. I always have been."

Elsa wasn't sure if it was the tone of his voice or the fact that he had journeyed so far to find her, but something inside her gave way. Her eyes filled with tears. "I'm sorry I revealed my powers the way I did. I didn't mean to scare you. I don't want to hurt anyone."

"I know that." He took her hand.

"The Duke was pressuring me, the coronation was starting, and I had just learned—" She stopped herself.

"Learned what?" Hans pressed.

Elsa pulled away. "Nothing." How could she explain Anna?

"I can't help you if you don't let me in," Hans said. She was quiet. "I think what you can do is breathtaking."

She looked at him. "You do?"

Hans smiled. "You've been given an incredible gift. Think of all you could do for Arendelle with your powers. The people are only scared because they don't understand your magic. If you show them how you can stop this winter and how your magic can protect the kingdom, they'll fall in line. You'll see."

"Fall in line?" Elsa repeated. She wasn't sure she liked the sound of that.

Hans appeared flustered. "You know what I mean. They'll respect your power the way they respect me for coming after you." He reached for her hand again. "Think of all we could do for the kingdom together."

Together. Elsa flinched. So that was it, wasn't it? Why hadn't she realized it before? Hans wasn't there for her; he was there for himself. "You still want to get married?"

He got down on one knee. "Yes, even with these powers, I want to marry you! Come back and accept your crown, and we can rule Arendelle together. You'll never have to be alone again. I promise you."

There it was again: *We can rule Arendelle together.* Hans coveted the throne. He didn't want her—he wanted power. "I'm sorry, but I can't marry you. And I am not going back with you, either." She started to ascend the staircase. "I'm sorry you came all this way for nothing."

"What?" Hans's face fell. "You have to come back!" His voice had a sharp edge to it. "Only a monster would refuse!" He caught himself, and his eyes widened. "I mean—"

"Please leave," she cut him off. *Monster.* Despite his pleas, Hans saw her the same way the Duke did.

"Come back with me. If you would just stop the winter . . . Bring back summer." He sounded frustrated. "Please?"

"Don't you see? I can't," Elsa told him. "I don't know how, so I'm staying here, where I can't hurt anyone. I'm sorry."

Hans's face was calm. "I see," he said softly. "If you can't fix things, maybe Anna can."

The wind whistling around the palace was the only sound.

Elsa stumbled in shock. "What did you say?"

Hans pulled a piece of parchment from his pocket and held it up. "I said, maybe Anna can bring back summer.

That's why you're up here, isn't it? You're looking for your sister. I read everything in the queen's letter."

Elsa froze. "How did you get that?"

"You dropped it in your haste to get away from the castle," Hans said as he read it over again. "I guess you found it the day of your coronation. Why else would you have had a magic ice meltdown?" He smiled smugly. "I can't say I blame you. If I learned I had a sister who had been hidden from me for years, I'd go a little mad, too."

"Who did you tell about that letter?" Elsa whispered.

"No one—for now," Hans said. "I was hoping you'd come back, marry me, and make this arrangement easy, but if you won't, at least I have another option."

Elsa grasped the ice railing in panic. "You wouldn't."

"As thirteenth in line in my own kingdom, I didn't stand a chance." Hans paced the floor. "I knew I'd have to marry into the throne somewhere, so when the Duke of Weselton told me about you and Arendelle, I was intrigued. But I could never get anywhere with you. You were always closed off, and now you've doomed yourself. Once I tell the people that you wouldn't return or bring back summer, they really will think you're a monster."

"No!" Elsa rushed down the staircase at him, and Hans drew his crossbow and brandished it at her. Elsa stopped short in surprise.

She didn't recognize the man standing in front of her. This wasn't the man who had courted her for a year, sent her flowers weekly, and patiently waited for her to decide on their future.

In truth, Hans was the monster.

How could she have been such a fool?

"Thankfully, we now know Arendelle has another heir to the throne," Hans said. "Once I show the people this letter and find Anna, they will be indebted to me for saving their lost princess. I *am* charming, so unlike you, Anna will probably want to marry me in an instant. Then all that will be left to do is kill you and bring back summer."

"You're no match for me," Elsa told him. She felt a familiar tingle in her fingers as she prepared to aim at him.

"Maybe not, but I'm the hero who will save Arendelle from destruction." Hans ran to the castle doors and opened them. "Guards! Guards! I've found the princess! She's armed!" He grinned at her. "Help me!"

Hans had tricked her. Anger bubbled up inside her as she raised her hands, a bright blue glow hovering above her fingers. "You won't get away with this!"

"I already have." Hans pointed the crossbow at the ceiling and fired. The bolt hit the enormous snowflake chandelier. Elsa watched in horror as it shattered and fell toward her. She tried to dive out of the way but wasn't quick enough. The crystals rained down on her, knocking her to the ground. By the time she got back up, she was face to face with Arendelle guards. Men who had dedicated their lives to protecting the crown were now holding swords aimed at their princess. Two larger men in red overcoats ran into the room behind them. Elsa recognized them immediately. They were the Duke of Weselton's men.

"We've got her!" one shouted. "Come quietly if you don't want to be hurt."

How dare they threaten her? They had no authority in this kingdom. Elsa's fingertips began to glow, and the two men raised their crossbows in unison.

"I'm not coming with you," Elsa told them. "Just stay back!"

She heard the crossbows before she saw them coming for her. She put up her hands, creating a wall of ice as a shield. Their bolts pierced the frozen surface, and it started to crack. Elsa ran around the wall, trying to find a way out of the palace. She needed to find Hans and keep him from getting away, but the men kept coming. Elsa fired again and again, building icy barriers around her.

"Go around!" one of the Duke's men shouted as he fought his way around daggers that sprung up from the floor. They came at her from opposite directions.

Elsa flung out her hands to protect herself. "I don't want to hurt you! Stay back!"

"Fire!" One of the men threw his crossbow to the other one.

Elsa shot a steady stream of snow until it froze like an icicle, pinning one man to the wall and holding him there. With her other hand, she shot another stream across the room, creating a wall of ice that pushed the Duke's other henchman into the next chamber, hiding him from her sight. Still, she kept pushing, thinking of Hans's betrayal and her sister, who was unknowingly the prince's target.

Her own guards ran into the room again.

"Princess Elsa!" one cried. "Don't be the monster they fear you are!"

At the word *monster*, she dropped her arms in defeat. One of the Duke's men took advantage of her hesitation and fired his crossbow again in her direction.

Angry, Elsa swirled her arms, and the walls around her crackled as new ice formed over old. Elsa imagined a great protector, and the ground began to shake. Ice flew around her fingers, spiraling like a cyclone until it formed a snow beast several stories tall. The beast's eyes glowed blue as it let out a ferocious growl.

"Go away!" it seemed to bark, although even Elsa couldn't be certain. It could have been the sound of the rumbling walls starting to fall around them. The guards raised their swords again and prepared to fight the beast.

Elsa took that moment to run for it. She burst through the palace doors into the snow and came face to face with more guards.

Fear entered their eyes as soon as they saw the giant snow beast. All of them raised their crossbows and aimed at her heart.

"Please." Elsa's voice was barely audible over the wind. "Let me explain."

They didn't listen. "Fire!"

Crossbow bolts flew toward her at the same moment the snow monster tumbled backward out of the palace, his icy left leg cut off. He lost his balance and crashed into the staircase, breaking through it and falling straight into the gorge. The remaining steps started to shake and tumble. Elsa tried to outrun the collapse, jumping before the steps fell into the gorge below. She fell down hard on the other side, ice crashing around her. Then the world faded to black.

CHAPTER TWENTY-THREE

Anna

The sun didn't come up the next morning. The kingdom was shrouded in darkness thanks to the swirling blizzard that continued to drop snow onto Arendelle at an alarming rate. With the poor conditions, it apparently took Kristoff much longer than it normally would to reach the Valley of the Living Rock.

"I don't understand," Kristoff muttered to himself. "We've been traveling for hours. We should be there by now." Kristoff pulled the sleigh to a halt.

"Are you lost?" Anna asked.

"You look lost!" Olaf commented.

Anna wouldn't blame him if he was. It was snowing so hard she couldn't see her hand in front of her face.

"Shhh!" Kristoff lifted the lantern off its hook and waved it into the darkness. Sven pawed the snow uneasily as Kristoff peered into the distance.

Anna saw it at the same time Kristoff did: several pairs of yellow eyes were looking back at them.

Wolves.

A distinct growl sounded in the distance and the pack of wolves emerged from the trees. Anna couldn't believe how sharp their fangs looked.

Kristoff placed the lantern back on the hook and grabbed the reins. "Sven! Go!" The sled lurched and Sven took off at top speed.

"Aww, look! Doggies! Aren't they cute?" Olaf said.

"They're not dogs, Olaf! What do we do?" Anna asked as Kristoff tried to stay ahead of the pack racing after the sleigh.

He reached behind their seat, grabbed a stick, and lit it from the lantern. It immediately flamed. "I can handle a few wolves," he said, waving the fire in the air.

"I want to help!" Anna shouted.

"No!" Kristoff cracked the reins harder.

"Why not?" They were moving so fast the falling snow felt like daggers hitting Anna's face.

"Because I don't trust your judgment," Kristoff snapped.

Anna set her shoulders. "Excuse me?"

"You're not thinking straight! Who keeps insisting on going out in this weather when they're clearly getting sick?" He kicked a wolf and it flew backward. Anna hadn't even seen the wolf coming.

She reached for something in the sleigh to use as a weapon. Olaf handed her Kristoff's lute. "I am not getting sick!"

"You keep passing out and mumbling to yourself," he reminded her.

"That's because I'm seeing things!" She swung the lute. It connected with a wolf, and the animal ran away.

"Whoa!" Kristoff actually looked impressed. "What kinds of things?"

Anna stopped swinging the lute and looked at him. "I know it sounds crazy, but I keep seeing myself with the princess when I was a little girl." Kristoff held the torch over the side to keep the wolves at bay. "I mean, I guess it's not entirely crazy. I'm pretty sure I was kissed by a troll once, but I don't remember it happening."

"You weren't kidding about that?" Kristoff's eyes widened. "Do you actually know Grand Pabbie?"

"Who is Grand Pabbie?" Anna asked as Kristoff singed a wolf about to land in the sleigh.

A second wolf snatched Kristoff's overcoat. Kristoff tumbled out of the sled before he could answer her question.

"Kristoff!" Anna screamed, grabbing the torch before it fell. There was no time to signal to Sven to stop, and if he did, they'd be done for.

"Here!" she heard Kristoff shout.

He was holding on to a rope that was dragging him behind the sleigh. The wolves were gaining on him. Anna lit the first thing she saw—Kristoff's sleeping sack.

"Ooh!" Olaf said as the fire ignited the bedding.

Anna picked it up and tossed it out the back of the sled. Kristoff screamed as the flames shot toward him, narrowly missing his head.

The wolves retreated, then came racing back again.

Anna rushed to the back of the sleigh to help him up. Kristoff was already pulling himself in.

"You almost set me on fire!"

"Guys?" Anna heard Olaf say, but she ignored him.

She pulled Kristoff the rest of the way in. "But I didn't!"

"Guys?" Olaf tried again. "We've reached the end of the path!"

Kristoff and Anna both did a double take. A ravine was a half a mile in front of them and Sven was barreling toward it, spurred on by the sound of the wolves. Anna and Kristoff hurried to the front of the sleigh.

"Get ready to jump, Sven!" Anna shouted.

Kristoff picked up Olaf and threw him into Anna's lap, then lifted them both his arms.

"Hey!" Anna protested.

Kristoff tossed her forward, and she landed on Sven's back with Olaf in her arms. "You don't tell him what to do! I do!" Kristoff cut the line from the sled just as they reached the ravine. "Jump, Sven!"

Sven leapt into the air. Anna looked back in a panic for Kristoff. He and his sled were already airborne. Sven landed on the other side of the ravine, almost pitching Anna and Olaf off him as he came to a grinding halt. Anna jumped off and raced back to the edge of the cliff. Kristoff leapt off the sled as it plummeted into the ravine. She watched in horror as he attempted to reach the other side, instead hitting the edge of the cliff and sliding backward.

"Hang on!" she shouted. "Rope! I need rope!" Anna called in a panic to Olaf, but she knew everything they needed was in that sleigh. *Please don't let anything happen to Kristoff,* she silently begged.

Suddenly, a pickax with rope attached to it flew through the air above her head. The ax hit the ground in front of Kristoff.

"Grab on!" someone yelled.

Anna looked up. A man with red hair and a blue overcoat was holding the other end of the rope.

"Help me pull him up!" he told her.

Anna grabbed the rope, dug in her heels, and helped pull Kristoff to safety. He collapsed on his back, breathing heavily. She was so relieved she thought about hugging him, but she stopped herself and gave Kristoff a moment to catch his breath. Now probably wasn't the time to bring up how his newly paid-off sleigh had gone up in flames.

Anna looked up at their rescuer, who stood next to a pale golden horse. "Thank you. If you hadn't come along when you did—"

He cut her off. "Of course." They both knew what would have happened if he hadn't arrived. "What are you all doing out here in the middle of this storm? It's dangerous with the wolves and the weather."

"My thoughts exactly," Kristoff said, breathing heavily, "but once this one has an idea in her head, she has to go with it. I am the fool who listened."

Anna held out her hand to shake the strangers. "I'm Anna, and the one you helped rescue is Kristoff."

"I wouldn't exactly say 'rescue,'" Kristoff mumbled.

The man blinked his hazel eyes several times before he spoke. "Did you say you're *Anna*?"

"Yes, we saw the deep freeze happen in Harmon and headed down to Arendelle to see what was going on," she explained, talking a mile a minute. "But then the wolves caught up with our sleigh and we reached a ravine and had to jump and Kristoff threw me onto Sven—that's his reindeer—and then he jumped, but his sled didn't make it. He almost didn't, either, but then you came along." She smiled brightly. The man still looked incredibly bewildered. "But we're all safe now. I'm Anna. Did I say that already?"

He squeezed her hand and smiled. "You did, but that's okay."

He had a great smile.

"It's a pleasure to meet you, Anna. I'm Hans of the Southern Isles."

Anna gripped his hand tight. "You're Hans? *The* Prince Hans?"

He laughed. "Yes. I think so. And you're *the* Anna. Am I right?"

"Uhh . . . yes!" He was funny. Anna laughed at the absurdness of it all. The wolves were on the other side of the ravine, Kristoff was safe, and they had somehow found Elsa's Prince Hans. It had to be fate!

"Prince Hans!" Olaf ran out of the woods, where he'd been gathering some of Kristoff's things that had flown through the air. "It's you! It's really you!"

Hans lost his footing in the snow.

"Oh, it's all right," Anna said, over the shock of a talking snowman by then. "Princess Elsa made him. His name is

Olaf, and he's trying to help us find Elsa so we can stop this winter."

"We're looking for her now!" Olaf added.

"You are?" Hans looked surprised when she and Olaf nodded.

Kristoff sat up and Anna dropped Hans's hand. "Great," Kristoff said. "Now that we're all clear on who's who, we should get moving before the wolves come back. Thanks for your help, *Prince* Hans."

Anna blushed at Kristoff's sarcasm. She was used to it, but Hans was a prince. "Sorry, it's been a long few days. We haven't had any luck finding Princess Elsa so far. Have you seen any sign of her?"

Hans's face fell. "No, I haven't. Have you?"

Anna shook her head. "No. We believe she may be in the Valley of the Living Rock, but with all this snow, we can't seem to find it."

"Really?" Prince Hans ran a hand through his hair. "I thought she was headed to the North Mountain—that's why I came this way—but I've seen no sign of her. I doubt she made it up there, anyway."

"Why do you say that?" Kristoff asked.

Hans gave him a look. "She's a princess. Do you really think she made it up the North Mountain with no supplies?"

Anna hesitated. She hadn't thought of it that way before,

but she wasn't convinced. After all, she and Olaf had come this far, and she'd never left Harmon a day in her life. Wouldn't Elsa be able to make it up a mountain with the aid of her powers?

"It's not impossible." Kristoff seemed to hear her thoughts. He stood between her and Hans. "She can make snow, so we know she likes cold places."

So now Kristoff is on Elsa's side? Anna wondered. *Didn't he just call her ice crazy last night?*

"Olaf? You mean the talking snowman." Hans seemed perturbed as he gave Olaf a small wave. "Hello there."

"Prince Hans! It's so good to finally meet you!" Olaf said, clapping his twigs. "I love your flowers!" Hans looked confused.

"Olaf told us how you sent the princess purple heather every week," Anna said. "He said you were one of the only people who could convince her to leave her room."

Hans blushed. Or maybe it was just windburn. "It was her favorite flower. They always seemed to cheer her up." His face clouded over. "Princess Elsa didn't trust many people. I knew she was unhappy, but I never thought she'd plunge Arendelle into an eternal winter."

"It had to be an accident," Anna said as a gust of wind sent snow swirling their way. "She wouldn't have done something like this to her kingdom on purpose."

"Have you ever met the princess?" Hans asked. Anna and Kristoff shook their heads. "I knew her well," he said softly. "She was conflicted, and sometimes very angry. She was having a tough time with this coronation."

"It's true," Olaf chimed in. "Elsa wasn't happy about her hair. They wanted her to wear it up, and she said, 'Olaf, should I wear it down?' And I said, 'I don't have any hair.'" He pointed to the twigs on his head.

"She was upset about the crown." Hans corrected him. "She kept telling me she wasn't ready to be a queen. I thought she was just having pre-coronation jitters, but she was insistent. She told me she didn't want to be responsible for the whole kingdom. I tried to reassure her that she'd be a good ruler, and that I'd be there for her, but . . ."

Anna touched his arm. "It sounds like you tried to help her."

"I hated seeing her so upset." He looked away. "The morning of her coronation, I tried to calm her down, but she got angry with me and some of the castle staff. The Duke of Weselton, too. She kept telling us to stay back. That's when . . ." Hans shut his eyes tight. "We barely made it out of that hallway alive."

"She tried to hurt you?" Anna was shocked. Would the princess really try to hurt the man she loved?

"Ice can be dangerous," Kristoff said. "I should know.

I deliver ice for a living. It's beautiful, but it's also powerful and has a magic that can't always be controlled."

"Exactly. And like I said, she was angry," Hans said. "She shot ice straight at us, trying to pierce our hearts." He looked directly at Anna. "The Duke barely got away."

"I wouldn't be surprised if that guy provoked her," Kristoff said with a chuckle. "He seemed real friendly when we met him."

"The Duke was almost killed," Hans said sharply. "How friendly would you be? I'm sorry, but the princess we thought we knew is gone. The one I saw that day is a . . . monster."

Elsa wouldn't abandon her people, would she? Anna felt a sharp pang and held her head. She was getting another flash. But this time it wasn't a forgotten memory. Instead, she felt pain. *Help me!* she heard someone cry out. *Anna! Help me!*

"Elsa?" Anna whispered, and crumbled to the ground.

Kristoff reached for her, but Hans caught her first. Her eyes fluttered open and closed, his face going into and out of focus.

"The princess is in trouble," Anna said. "I can feel it."

Kristoff pulled Anna out of Hans's grasp. "You are going home. Now." He looked at Hans. "She fell ill yesterday but tried to push on. She's too stubborn for her own good. She needs to get inside and rest."

The pain subsided as quickly as it had come, and Anna shrugged away. "It's just a headache. I can keep going. I have to get to the valley. I don't know why, but I feel like Elsa could be in danger."

"Danger?" Olaf looked frightened.

"Valley?" Hans questioned.

"Olaf thought she was on the North Mountain, but now he seems to think she's in the Valley of the Living Rock," Kristoff explained. He looked at Hans sharply. "Ever hear her mention it?"

Hans thought for a moment. "No, I'm afraid not." He looked at Anna. "But if you think she's there and she's in trouble, we have to find her. I only have my horse, Sitron, but I have money and things to barter. We can get you a horse, too, and then we'll locate this valley together."

"And convince her to come back with us and help her people," Anna added. She took a deep breath and tried to steady herself. The pain was gone, but the memory of Elsa's voice lingered. What was happening to her?

"Yes," Hans agreed. "And if she doesn't want the crown, she can abdicate, but she must bring back summer."

"Whoa!" Kristoff interrupted and appealed to Anna. "You cannot go to the valley in this condition." He touched her arm. "Anna, something is going on with you. I don't know what it is, but you need rest."

Anna set her jaw. "Someone has to stop this winter, and I feel like . . . it's *me*."

"But you don't even know her," Kristoff reminded her. "What if the prince is right? If she's that angry, she might hurt you."

"She won't," Anna insisted. The wind was whipping hard in the open clearing, and she felt her balance falter. Hans offered her his elbow to help her stay upright. "Kristoff, I can't go home now. Arendelle needs help. I have to try to do something."

"I agree," Hans said.

"Who asked you?" Kristoff said, and Sven snorted. Kristoff looked at Anna. "This is crazy! You can't just go off with this guy you just met!"

"I went with you, didn't I?" Anna reminded him. Kristoff was quiet.

"Excuse me, but I don't think you should be yelling at the lady," Hans said. "Anna seems smart and knowledgeable. She's trying to help save the kingdom."

"Thank you," Anna said.

Hans wasn't brooding or indecisive. He might have been worried Elsa wouldn't return with him, but he was still willing to go after her. Maybe he'd be able to talk sense into her. Something told her she needed to be with Hans when he found her.

"Anna, see reason! We've lost all our supplies, my sleigh is in pieces, and this weather is making everyone a little crazy." Kristoff was growing agitated now. "You can't possibly want to keep going when we don't even know for sure where Elsa is! We're going with a snowman's hunch!"

"We do know! When the letter was read aloud, I heard someone say 'the Valley of the Living Rock'," Olaf reminded them.

"You heard me read the letter?" Hans said slowly.

"It was you!" Olaf said happily. "I should've known. You're so good to Elsa."

"Anna," Kristoff tried again. "Don't do this."

Why couldn't he see how important this was? She couldn't show up back home and tell her parents she had failed. Harmon would never survive this eternal winter.

But that was the problem, wasn't it? Harmon wasn't Kristoff's village; it was hers. Kristoff just passed through with ice deliveries. He didn't care about the people the way she did. The only one he cared about was Sven. "I'm going," she said firmly. "And I have no problem going the rest of the way with Hans. So . . . are you going to come with us?"

Kristoff threw up his hands. "Look, I know the valley well, and even I can't find it in this weather—and *I'm* not getting sick. We should all turn back."

"I'm still going," she said firmly. "Hans is, too. We can all go."

"No. I think you three have it covered on your own. I'm going to salvage what's left of my sleigh. Come on, Sven." He turned his back and stalked off.

Sven grunted mournfully as he looked from Anna to Kristoff.

"It's okay, Sven," Anna said, surprised she couldn't change Kristoff's mind. "You look after him. I'll be okay." She watched the reindeer follow Kristoff into the woods.

"I'm going to miss them," Olaf said sadly.

Me too, Anna thought.

Hans shook his head. "I can't believe he'd leave you out here."

"I'll be fine," Anna said firmly.

"I don't doubt it. You seem like a natural leader." Hans was looking at her so intently Anna started to blush. He pointed at smoke in the distance. "There has to be a cabin that way. Let's find shelter for the night." He held out his hand to help her onto his horse. Anna climbed on and Hans placed Olaf in front of her. Then he mounted the horse behind them.

"We're going to make a good team, Anna. I can feel it."

"So can I," Anna said with a soft smile.

Team. She liked the idea of that.

CHAPTER TWENTY-FOUR

Elsa

Elsa felt her head pounding before she opened her eyes.

Why did her head hurt?

Then she remembered: Hans revealing his sinister nature, her desperate attempt to get away before Hans could find Anna on his own, the ice chandelier crashing and almost impaling her, and the ambush outside her fortress. If only she'd known they were planning to take her back to Arendelle Castle and lock her away.

She sat up and the blanket that had been lying over her fell, revealing chains. Elsa wore metal gloves, meant to keep her from using her hands—or, more specifically, her magic. The chains were anchored to a large boulder on the floor that prevented her from moving more than a few feet. She pulled on the chains, hoping to yank them free, but it was no use.

Once again, she was a prisoner in her own castle.

The chains were only long enough to allow her to walk to the castle window. Outside, Arendelle wasn't just covered in snow; it was buried. Layers of snow were piled so high past rooftops that houses were no longer visible. She heard a crash and wondered what had fallen: A house? A statue? A ship? She could see the boats out in the harbor, frozen where they were anchored, and she could do nothing to change it. It seemed the more she panicked, the bigger the storm got. As she felt her fingertips tingle, icicles grew like weeds in the dungeon, causing the walls to groan with misery.

Where were all the people? How were they staying warm? She thought again of the mother and baby she had frightened in the castle courtyard on coronation day. Were they safe?

Was Anna?

Elsa closed her eyes, overcome with worry. "What have I done?" she whispered.

Mama, Papa, please help me break this curse, she pleaded. *The kingdom can't survive much longer. Help Anna remember who she really is!*

As she suspected, no answers came.

She would have to figure this out on her own. The only way she could do that was escape. Maybe if she could get word to Anna without actually going near her, she could jog her memory. If only she had that letter as proof of the truth. Elsa concentrated on her cuffs and they started to glow. *Break,* she willed them. *Break!* Instead, the cuffs started to freeze up, making it almost impossible to move.

The situation seemed hopeless.

"Princess Elsa?"

Elsa looked up. Lord Peterssen was peering at her through a barred window in the dungeon door.

"Lord Peterssen!" she cried. The ice on her cuffs stopped forming immediately. She rushed to the door but was yanked back by her chains.

"Are you all right?" he asked, holding tightly to the bars.

Aside from Olaf, Lord Peterssen was the only other person in her life who treated her like family. Her father had trusted him with his life. Maybe she could do the same. "No. I need to find someone. Desperately. Lord Peterssen, did my parents ever talk about having another child? A girl? Younger than me, with red hair? Her name is Anna?"

For the briefest of seconds, she thought she saw Lord Peterssen's brown eyes flicker. "I . . . the name does sound familiar."

"Yes!" Elsa tried harder to yank the chains out of the wall so she could get closer to him. "Do you remember her?"

"I'm sorry. I don't know who you're talking about," he

said as the wind howled fiercely. "You are the only heir to this kingdom."

"But I'm not," Elsa stressed. "Lord Peterssen, please! I must find this girl. She'd be a few years younger than me. We need to start a search! I must find her before Prince Hans does."

"Prince Hans?" Lord Peterssen appeared puzzled.

"Yes. You cannot trust him! He does not have the best interests of the kingdom at heart." She longed to say more, but didn't want to scare him off. "I know my word doesn't hold much weight at the moment, but you must believe me."

"No one can search for anyone in this weather," he said. "We are running out of firewood, and food is growing scarce. The people are freezing! They're getting desperate. Prince Hans went after you, but he has not returned."

"Where is he?" Elsa's cuffs started to glow again.

"No one knows, and we can't send anyone out to look for him. This cold isn't even safe for our livestock," Lord Peterssen told her. "The men who brought you here are the only ones who have made it back. Unfortunately, the Duke met them before I did, and he convinced them to lock you in this dungeon." She saw his eyes flash angrily. "The men were scared after what happened at your ice palace. I only just learned you were down here. The Duke will pay for claiming authority in a land where he has none."

"Then you will set me free?" Elsa asked, yanking harder to pull off her cuffs. They glowed brighter. "I can help."

"I've searched everywhere for the key to this room but cannot find it," Lord Peterssen told her.

Elsa tried not to be disappointed. "I know you will find it. You have always been there for me."

"I've always thought you'd make a fine leader. We need you to lead us now," Lord Peterssen said. "Will you bring back summer? We can't hold on much longer."

Elsa's arms drooped to her sides. "I truly don't know how."

"You are your father's daughter," Lord Peterssen said with resolve. His eyes searched hers. "I know you can dig deep inside yourself and figure out a way to stop this storm. We've been patient, but we need you now more than ever."

Be patient. She heard Grand Pabbie in her head.

A storm was raging outside and growing fiercer. The time for patience had passed. She needed Anna's memories to return and the curse to end. That might be the only way they could save Arendelle and the kingdom: they needed to do it together. "I know," Elsa told him. "I want to stop this winter badly, but I can't do it alone. I need to find someone who can help me."

"Princess, we can't—"

"Stop right there!"

There was a commotion in the hallway and then shouting. Lord Peterssen was ripped away from the bars. Elsa couldn't see anything from her vantage point. Suddenly, she glimpsed the top of someone's head. A white toupee flapped in the wind.

"Lift me up!" she heard someone cry.

His face appeared in the bars on her window. "Princess Elsa," the Duke of Weselton announced, "you are a threat to Arendelle. You are going nowhere."

CHAPTER TWENTY-FIVE

Anna

Hans collected fresh supplies and borrowed a second horse for Anna from the people in the cabin they found. The couple insisted they stay overnight before continuing on their journey. After all they had seen with the summer snowstorm, the appearance of Olaf didn't frighten them at all. By morning, they were begging them not to press on.

"These mountain trails are treacherous even in the most optimal conditions," the man told them. "And this weather will make it impossible."

"It's hailing now, too," the wife added. "Please, Prince Hans, if you are who you say you are, go back to Arendelle."

"Maybe they're right," Hans said, looking out their cabin windows. All they could see was white. "The storm is getting worse. Soon we won't be able to get back to Arendelle at all."

"We have to keep going," Anna insisted. "You know as well as I do the only way to stop this winter is to find Princess Elsa."

I want to bake my own cookie for Papa! she heard a child's voice say in her head. *Wait for Miss Olina,* another person said.

Who was "Miss Olina"?

"And what if she doesn't want to be found?" Hans asked as the couple added the last of their wood to the fireplace. "You don't want to hear this, but Elsa is only thinking of herself. She probably wants to hold the kingdom prisoner."

Prisoner. Anna's head seared with pain and she saw a blond woman chained to a wall, snow falling all around. She was hurting. *Elsa?*

"What's the matter?" Hans asked.

"Nothing." She held back from telling Hans what she was seeing. "I've just got a slight headache."

"Maybe that friend of yours was right—this weather is too much on you." Hans sounded slightly annoyed. "We should turn back to Arendelle before it's impossible to travel. You can shelter at the castle with me till the storm passes."

"It's not going to pass," Anna reminded him. *Not until I help her stop the storm.*

She held her breath. What had made her think that? There was another flash, and she saw herself as a little girl sledding across a room full of ice. Why was she seeing memories of moments she couldn't recall?

Hans frowned. "You're probably right. I think Elsa wants Arendelle to suffer."

"No! The princess wouldn't do that, would she?" the wife asked.

For a man who was supposedly in love with Elsa, Hans had a funny way of showing it. And as charming as he could be, he really did like to rehash the same point over and over.

"No," Anna said, getting aggravated. "I think the princess is frightened. If we could just talk to her, I'm sure we could work this out before the situation worsens. That's why we need to find her quickly and keep going," Anna stressed.

Hans sighed. "I don't want to see you get hurt."

"Elsa would never hurt Anna," Olaf interrupted. "She loves her more than anything."

Anna and Hans looked at the snowman. A gust of wind blew the door open, knocking Olaf's head off. The husband and wife rushed to bolt it shut again.

"Hey, do me a favor and grab my butt," Olaf's head said to Hans.

Anna was lost in her own thoughts.

Olaf.

Her new memories.

The voices.

All those things felt like a tiny itch between her shoulders that she couldn't reach.

Why had she always dreamed of snow?

Why did she make snowman cookies?

Why did she feel such a pull to Arendelle?

Maybe because she was always supposed to be there at that exact moment to help Elsa. She and Elsa seemed to have a connection Anna didn't understand. She needed to find the princess and find out why.

There was a sudden pounding on the door. Everyone looked at one another. Hans reached for his sheath.

"Open it," he instructed the man.

A guard in a green uniform fell through the door.

"My goodness!" the wife cried as she and Anna rushed forward to help him up. The husband struggled to close the door again against the wind.

The guard saw Hans and his eyes widened. "Prince Hans! We've been looking for you everywhere." His voice was hoarse and his face was red with windburn. "When we didn't see you after the battle, we thought we'd lost you. I planned to keep looking, but my horse is struggling in this cold. I saw the cabin and—"

The husband started putting on layers of clothing. "I'll

get your horse in the barn," he said, and pulled on his boots before going to the door.

"What battle?" Anna asked.

Hans ignored her and helped the man to the fire. "What's happened? Is everything all right in Arendelle?"

The wife wrapped the guard in a blanket. He took it gratefully as he shivered. He looked at the people around him, then back at Hans. "May we speak in private?"

"Of course," the wife said, and put her arm around Anna. "Come, dear. We should see if we can find you some warmer clothes."

But Anna didn't want to go. Now wasn't the time for secrets.

"Is everything all right?" Anna asked the men. "What aren't you telling us?"

Hans hesitated. "The North Mountain has suffered an avalanche. I don't want to upset you when you've given up so much to be here, but I don't know if we can continue toward the valley with the situation outside so precarious." The guard looked at him.

Hans was charming, but there was something about him she wasn't sure she trusted.

Anna was about to argue, but she suddenly felt it in her aching bones—the castle was calling to her. Elsa wasn't in the valley anymore, and she'd long ago left the North

Mountain. She wasn't sure how she knew this, but she wasn't about to share her feeling.

"Let's go back to Arendelle," she agreed. "We can wait out the storm in the castle. Maybe when we're there, we'll find a clue we're missing."

"Yay! Elsa will be so excited to see you!" Olaf said, and Hans looked at him. "She's been looking for you forever." Anna didn't flinch.

Hans smiled. "I meant what I said before—you'd be a great leader."

"I don't know about that," Anna said.

Hans didn't break his stare. "I do. Let's get you to Arendelle so you can see that for yourself."

CHAPTER TWENTY-SIX

Kristoff

"It's official! I've decided something, Sven," Kristoff told his friend as they trudged down the ravine to find what was left of his sleigh. "Who needs people when I have a reindeer?"

Sven grunted. The reindeer was too busy watching the darkening tree line for signs of another wolf attack. Fortunately, between the light of the rising moon and the bright snow, Kristoff and Sven could see pretty far into the distance.

There was no reason to look back.

So he'd let Anna go off with some smooth-talking prince and a snowman to find a princess who didn't want finding. He wasn't about to get himself and Sven killed over it.

Yes, he wanted to bring back summer—all this

available ice made selling it for a living kind of hard—but he was used to the weather. He spent most days up in the mountains, being covered in snow, wool clothing, and heavy boots that smelled of sweat. And it didn't matter what he smelled like, because who was around to smell him? Only Sven. Well, reindeer didn't smell that great, either. So bring on an eternal winter. He could handle it.

But Anna . . . the cold was clearly getting to her. He'd chalked it up to hypothermia or possibly frostbite, but deep down he knew that wasn't it. It was almost as if the closer she got to finding Princess Elsa, the more connected she was to her. Like magic.

Let people make fun of magic all they wanted. He knew it was real.

He'd been raised around magic his whole life.

Not that he'd tell Anna that. Why would he when she was so infuriating? She talked on and on *and on*, not just to him and Sven—to everyone she met!

She was also impulsive and strong-minded, which was how he'd allowed himself to be talked into taking her to Arendelle in the first place. Feisty-pants thought she could stop an eternal winter even though she had no idea how to find Elsa or what she'd say to make her end the madness.

Kristoff could see the wreck of his sleigh as they approached the bottom of the ravine. He was almost afraid to see how bad the damage was. Instead, he concentrated on Sven. "I've decided all people want to do is use you and cheat you." He used his reindeer voice again: "You're right. They're all bad! Except you."

He rubbed Sven's snout. "Aww, thanks, buddy. Let's see what we can salvage here."

He looked at the sled and sighed. His beloved ride was in a million pieces. His lute was destroyed. His ice ax must have gone flying, because it wasn't among the wreckage. The little food they'd had had already been scavenged by critters. There wasn't much to salvage, but Kristoff examined every item to make sure. Finally, he climbed onto Sven.

"Now what do we do, Sven? I didn't think I could find the valley, but we don't really have a choice. We have to get you out of this weather too, buddy." He looked around at the landscape. "We've got to be close. We'll find it."

Sven wouldn't budge. He snorted loudly.

"Yes, I'm sure she's fine. They probably made their way to a cabin. I saw smoke in the distance," Kristoff told him. "We are *not* joining them there. Let's go. Stop worrying."

Sven gave him a withering look.

"You don't want to help her anymore?" Kristoff said in his Sven voice.

"Of course I don't want to help her anymore!" Kristoff pulled on Sven's reins and they started their ascent up the ravine. "In fact, this whole thing has ruined me for helping anyone ever again."

As they climbed, an angry snow squall descended, causing almost whiteout conditions. Going home was the wise choice. But that meant he was going to the same place Anna was headed.

Sven snorted again.

"Yes, I know that's where she's headed." Sven gave him a look. "Okay, so maybe I do look like a jerk showing up there now when we could have all gone together."

Sven snorted louder.

"He wasn't a total stranger—he's Elsa's prince." Kristoff rolled his eyes. "So *of course* he did the right thing and agreed to go with her." He thought for a moment. "Okay, yeah. I was a jerk."

Sven pranced around while Kristoff stood there feeling guilty.

"So now what? We go find her? Or we get to the valley and apologize?"

Sven looked at him.

"Yeah, we won't find her again in this. We'll go to the valley and then I'll apologize when she arrives, okay? I get it. I screwed up."

Kristoff spent the entire journey to the valley consumed with self-hatred. Anna was out there in this weather with a total stranger. He'd abandoned her when she'd needed him. No wonder Bulda thought he'd never find a girl.

The snow was falling heavier and wetter than it had earlier, but at least the journey was quiet. Without Anna, there was no one to tell him what to do, or talk incessantly about her favorite food (hers was sandwiches), or almost set him on fire.

Maybe he did miss having company. Even Olaf.

Not that he'd tell Sven that.

It took several hours to get to the Valley of the Living Rock, but Kristoff knew the route like the back of his callused hands. Even under all that snow, he was able to spot the peculiar rock formations that marked the location of his home. When they got closer, Kristoff jumped off Sven and they walked up the path of boulders until they arrived at the valley.

The second they were inside the valley, the snow stopped. The air warmed. The ground smelled like fresh dew and was covered with grassy moss. Kristoff descended the path into the fog and watched the rocks start to roll at the sight of him. Sven pranced eagerly, his tongue sticking out of his mouth. Kristoff tapped his knees, beckoning the rocks closer. A large number of them started to roll in his direction. They came to a stop and began to unfurl.

"Kristoff's home!" shouted Bulda, a female troll who

was front and center. His adoptive mother held her arms out for a hug. Kristoff stepped closer and she wrapped herself around his legs. The red gems around her neck seemed to have grown since the last time he visited. Several of them glowed, making her mossy-green dress look almost orange.

Dozens of other trolls unfurled from their rocky slumber and cheered. They clambered over one another to see him. "Yay! Kristoff's home!" they shouted.

The trolls had been his family ever since he was a small child. Life in an orphanage was no place for a free spirit like him. Whenever he could, he'd snuck out and followed the Arendelle ice harvesters up the mountain to see how they worked. On one such trip, he found Sven, and they became inseparable. After that, he didn't want to go back to the orphanage. Sven and ice were his new life. He was even earning a living! But one summer night, he was working with Sven when they saw a different kind of ice. It was crackling and glowing on the grassy mountainside. He and Sven were curious, so they followed the strange path up the mountain. It led them straight to the Valley of the Living Rock. Bulda spotted him and adopted him and Sven on the spot. Come to think of it, he never had asked her why that ice had appeared in the middle of the summer like that.

"Let me look at you!" Bulda said, beckoning him to stoop down to her level. Kristoff took a knee. "Are you hungry?" she asked. "I just made a stone soup. I'll fetch you a cup."

"No," Kristoff said quickly. He hated stone soup. Impossible to swallow. "I just ate. It's great to see you all. Have you had any visitors?" He looked around for Anna.

"No one but you!" Bulda said. "Why, are you expecting someone?"

If he told her he was expecting a girl to be there, he'd never hear the end of it. "No, but . . . where is Grand Pabbie?"

"He's napping," said one of Kristoff's little cousins. "But look! I grew a mushroom!" He showed off the mushroom growing on his mossy back.

"I earned my fire crystal," said another, holding up a glowing red stone.

"I passed a kidney stone," said one of his uncles, holding up the rock as proof.

"If you aren't hungry for my cooking, what brings you home?" Bulda asked.

Nothing got past her.

"I just wanted to see you, that's all," Kristoff lied.

Bulda studied him carefully, then looked at the others. "This is about a girl!"

The others cheered in agreement.

"No, no, no! You've got this all wrong!" Kristoff said even as his face grew red.

Sven snorted loudly, and several trolls gathered round as he pawed at the dirt and made noises.

"It *is* about a girl!" Bulda exclaimed, and the others chimed in again.

Kristoff rolled his eyes. "Guys, please! I've got bigger problems than finding a girl. The whole kingdom is covered in—"

"Snow?" Bulda said. "We know. But we want to hear about you!"

Kristoff gaped. "How do you know about the snow?"

Bulda ignored his question. "If you like this girl, why didn't she come home with you? Did your grumpiness scare her off?"

"No," he argued. "This isn't about me. I—"

"You tell this girl that she'll never met a fellow as sensitive and as sweet as my Kristoff!"

Now he felt even worse. "This is not about me and this girl! It's about Arendelle! I know you can't see it from inside your cocoon here, but it's not just the land outside the valley covered in snow. It's the whole kingdom! And it's the middle of the summer!" His family stood there, blinking. "If you know how to stop it, tell me!"

One of his little cousins pulled on Bulda's dress. "I thought Grand Pabbie said we couldn't tell anyone that she was here." Bulda made a face. "What? Didn't he say it was a secret?"

"Anna? She was here? With the prince? When did they leave?" he said hurriedly.

A large rock rolled forward, and Grand Pabbie unfurled from his slumber. He reached out for Kristoff and took his hands.

"Kristoff, you came! And just in time, I fear," he said, his voice gravelly.

"Where is Anna now? Is she okay? Was she mad at me?" he asked sheepishly and looked at Bulda. "I know I shouldn't have left her, okay? We're having a blizzard in the middle of the summer. It's not normal."

Sure, he'd acted like the snow was no big deal, but even an ice expert like him could see it was getting too cold to survive. When he'd last looked at the fjord, he'd seen the ships leaning and cracking. Soon buildings would do the same. There would be nowhere safe to shelter.

What would happen to Anna?

"So where is she now? What did you tell Anna?"

Grand Pabbie's brow furrowed. "Anna? You mean Princess Elsa. She's the one that came to see me."

"Not Anna?" Kristoff asked, feeling weak.

"No. Princess Elsa. I tried to help her—in what little way I can, given the curse."

"Curse?" Kristoff repeated. This was a lot to take in.

"She's in grave danger," Grand Pabbie said. "You must find her, Kristoff."

"Princess Elsa?" he asked. Grand Pabbie was confusing him. "I tried! No one knows where she is—although I met this talking snowman who knows the princess. And Anna and Prince Hans—Elsa's prince—were headed here." He looked at the valley opening again. "I thought they'd be here when I arrived."

"Anna isn't coming," Grand Pabbie said. "She's on her way back to Arendelle."

Kristoff stepped back in surprise. "You know who Anna is?"

"Anna's heart must be protected," Grand Pabbie said. "This is a precarious time for her."

"I know," Kristoff agreed. "I'm worried she's getting sick, but she's determined to keep going and find Princess Elsa."

"Kristoff, you must listen to me," he said. "There is a reason Anna feels drawn to Elsa and is fighting so hard to find her. Their connection is stronger than you think."

"I've sensed that," Kristoff admitted. "Ever since we journeyed to Arendelle, Anna's been feeling things . . . having strange headaches, and this talking snowman of Princess Elsa's knows her. None of it makes sense."

"Is she?" Grand Pabbie scratched his chin. "This

is good. She's starting to remember a past that has been hidden from her and Elsa for far too long."

"Past?" Kristoff asked, a new recollection dawning on him. It was as if he were awakening from a slumber himself, one that had kept him from knowing exactly how Anna and Elsa were connected. "Wait a minute. . . ."

Grand Pabbie patted his hand. "Yes. Anna and Elsa are sisters."

"Anna is a princess?"

"The curse that has prevented the sisters from being together is fading! Elsa already remembers who Anna is, but Anna's path has not been so simple. Love can thaw any curse," he insisted, "but until she regains her memories, Anna and Elsa cannot be near each other. This is very important! She must remember Elsa before they ever come face to face."

Kristoff felt his heart practically stop. Anna wouldn't quit till she found Elsa. "Why?"

"We don't have much time together, so I won't waste it trying to explain the past, but it has to do with the curse," Grand Pabbie explained. "If Anna gets near Elsa before she remembers their connection, Elsa's powers will turn her to ice."

"What?" Kristoff's voice sounded hollow to him.

"Their love for each other is so strong this curse is

already fading. Elsa remembers her past, but Anna is not there yet. Until the spell is broken, Anna must be kept away." Grand Pabbie frowned. "Elsa knows this. It is why she has kept her distance. But I fear someone else knows the truth, and is leading Anna into danger. Kristoff, Anna is headed to Arendelle, and Elsa is there too."

Kristoff paled. "Which means . . . I have to stop her!" Sven started to snort wildly and jump around. "Sven!" Kristoff shouted, climbing the steps double-time as he started running toward the valley's hidden exit. Sven galloped to meet him.

He didn't even think to say goodbye to Grand Pabbie, Bulda, or the others. Only one thing mattered now—saving Anna at all costs.

CHAPTER TWENTY-SEVEN

Anna

When Anna, Hans, and the guard arrived back in Arendelle, the kingdom was almost unrecognizable. In just two days, snow had drifted to the second story of the castle. The fire in the castle courtyard was long gone, and the fountain with the statue of the royal family was completely buried. They had to fight the wind to reach the castle doors, which were frozen over with ice. The guard had to pry them open with a pickax to get them inside.

A group was gathered in front of the fireplace, trying to keep warm, but it was clear they were shivering. The fire was almost out. Hans and the guard rushed to a group of guards and started talking while members of the castle staff busied themselves getting them blankets and warm clothes.

Anna couldn't move. Being inside the castle made the strange memories inside her head come on at full force.

A woman in an apron touched her arm. "Miss, are you all right?"

Anna gasped as a memory of herself with this woman flooded her mind. They were baking cookies in a large kitchen, and someone else was with them . . . a girl. Anna remembered burning her finger on the stove, and the girl freezing a pot of water so she could cool it down. *Elsa?* Anna clutched her heart and started to hyperventilate. Was this Miss Olina?

"Anna! Anna! Are you all right?" Hans rushed to her.

"Yes." Anna slowed her breathing. "I . . . just feel so strange. I . . ." The sudden memories didn't seem like dreams. They seemed like missing pieces of her life that she had somehow forgotten. She was desperate to figure out what was happening, but she was in a room of total strangers. If only Kristoff were with them. He'd help her make sense of it all.

"Where is Prince Hans?" someone cried. "Is he really here?" The Duke of Weselton pushed his way through the crowd. He was bundled up in a hat and several scarves. "Prince! Thank goodness you're alright. I was worried when my men said they couldn't find you after the battle."

"Where was this battle?" Anna asked. Her teeth were chattering. She felt so cold.

Hans still didn't answer her. "I'm fine," he told the Duke. "I got turned around in the snow."

The Duke turned to Anna and did a double take. "You!"

"We meet again." Anna rubbed her arms to keep warm. "Hello."

"You two know each other?" Hans asked, confused.

"Well, not exactly," Anna was saying when Olaf stepped forward and the Duke shrieked.

"Hi! I'm Olaf, and I like warm hugs," the snowman said. "I've brought Anna home! Wait till I tell Elsa! Is she here?"

Home? Anna thought.

"No one is permitted to see Princess Elsa!" the Duke declared. "She remains in the dungeons!"

"She's here?" Anna asked, but she felt her body fading. She was so tired.

A woman in a green uniform pushed her way to the front. "Prince Hans! You must do something! The Duke has the princess, and now he's taken away Lord Peterssen, too!"

"We demand Lord Peterssen be let out of his chambers!" a man in uniform cried.

They both started yelling at the Duke, but their voices were drowned out by the memories flooding Anna's mind.

A different woman in green, with a cap on her head, placed her hand on Anna's shoulder. "Are you all right?"

"Gerda?" Anna whispered, the name all of a sudden popping into her head.

The woman blinked in surprise. "Why, yes. How did you . . ."

A portly man with thinning hair appeared beside her.

Anna pointed shakily in his direction. "And you're Kai."

"Why, yes, miss," he said, looking at Gerda in confusion. "Can we get you warm clothes or glogg, perhaps? Olina doesn't have supplies to cook much else, I'm afraid."

"Olina," Anna repeated, seeing herself as a small girl in the kitchen with the palace cook again.

It was all too much for her to bear. She started to back away from the crowd and the people shouting for Lord Peterssen's release, looking for an escape.

"Miss?" Kai stepped forward, but Anna rushed through an open door.

She wandered into what appeared to be a portrait gallery. The large room had a slanted ceiling with blue panels and wooden beams. There was not much furniture—just a few benches and tables—and there were lots of paintings. Anna looked up at a portrait of a female knight in battle. For some reason, she could swear her name was Joan. As a matter of fact, all the portraits seemed familiar. Anna clutched her stomach in agony. Her hands were cold and she felt too weak to stand.

She didn't hear the door open behind her.

"Anna!"

Hans caught her as she started to collapse. He placed her on one of the benches, cradling her head as she sank into the velvet cushion. Anna couldn't breathe.

"What is happening to me?" she said in a panic.

"You're freezing! Hang on!" Hans stepped away to light a fire in the fireplace.

Anna kept talking. "I keep seeing things, hearing voices. . . . I know names of people I've never met before! Olaf remembers me, but I don't remember him . . . although I feel like I might." She looked up at Hans, her eyes full of tears. "I feel like I'm losing my mind."

He smiled gently. "It's all right. You're not losing your mind."

"I'm not?" Anna asked. Her teeth were chattering.

"No," he said, and put his hand on top of hers. "I think you're remembering your old life. The one you had before you were adopted." He looked at her intently. "I know this will be hard to understand, but the castle is your home."

"What?" Anna heard a whooshing sound in her ears. *I have to find Elsa.*

Hans continued. "You're an heir to this kingdom. Your

parents gave you up because Elsa struck you with her magic and almost killed you."

"No, I'm . . . no . . . Elsa wouldn't . . . she didn't . . ." Anna couldn't find the words to express what she was feeling. Something inside her was starting to crack. Hans wasn't making sense, and yet she knew he was telling the truth.

Do the magic! Do the magic! she heard a child say again with glee. That child was her.

"It's true," Hans insisted. "You don't remember, but I have the proof right here." He knelt down by her side and pulled a piece of parchment out of his jacket pocket. "This is a letter from the queen to Elsa telling her everything."

Anna's heart drummed faster. She reached for the letter. Hans held it away from her.

"Elsa is a threat to this kingdom and must be punished for her crimes, but your family legacy remains intact. You're the next in line for the throne! Don't you see?" Hans smiled eagerly. "With Elsa gone, summer will have to be restored! Then you and I can rule Arendelle together."

Anna tried to sit up. Her body was shaking, and such varied emotions were swirling that she thought she might implode. What was Hans saying? "I thought you loved Elsa . . . don't you?"

Hans's face fell as he rose to his full height. "As heir,

she was preferable, of course. But after what happened on her coronation day, there was no saving her. *You*, though . . . the long-lost princess of Arendelle—the people will adore you once they see their beloved queen's letter and realize who you are. Don't you see? My finding you before Elsa was fate."

"Elsa was looking for me? She's seen this letter?" Anna pulled herself up to stand and staggered toward him. "She knows she has a"—Anna played around with the word in her head before saying it aloud—"sister?" Her heart started beating even faster.

"Yes," Hans said. "I didn't tell you earlier because I was trying to protect you."

Anna heard the wind howling outside the large window, rattling the frame. The glass was iced over and she could see nothing but white outside.

She and Elsa were sisters?

If it was true, why couldn't she remember her life as a princess of Arendelle?

Why would her family have sent her away unless Hans was right that Elsa's magic almost killed her?

Anna closed her eyes tight, begging herself to remember, but nothing new came to her. Frustrated, she took it out on Hans. "So you learned Elsa tried to kill me and you were willing to lead me right toward her?"

Hans's eyes flickered in surprise. "I . . . The queen's letter said it was an accident, but . . ."

There was something he wasn't telling her. "Let me read the letter for myself, then."

Hans put the letter back in his pocket. "You're upset. Why don't you calm down first? I'll hold the letter for safekeeping."

She felt a flash of anger. "So instead of making things right with Elsa, you've been trying to sweet-talk me?" Hans's face reddened. "What is this battle everyone keeps talking about?" Hans shifted slightly. "And where is Elsa? If you know, why don't you let me talk to her so she can see for herself that the past is in the past? Maybe she'll stop this storm."

Hans's face was grim. "She's had her chance. I've tried talking to her—in her ice palace on the North Mountain, in fact. She isn't willing to negotiate, which means she's sentencing Arendelle and the rest of her kingdom to its doom. She knows all about you, but instead of helping you, she's cast you aside, just like she did Arendelle."

"She wouldn't do that," Anna argued.

Hans gestured to the frozen window, which was still rattling. "But she has. Look outside! We can't last much longer. The people are looking to me now for rescuing."

"How are you going to save them?" Anna scoffed. Hans

didn't say anything. "Wait. You're going to kill her?" Hans was still silent. "You c-can't!" she stuttered. "You have no right to decide her fate!"

Hans didn't flinch. "I'm the one saving this kingdom, and the people will thank me for it. I'm just sorry you won't be at my side when I do."

"You're no match for Elsa," Anna hissed as the rattling from the window grew louder.

"No, *you're* no match for Elsa," Hans countered. "I thought you might be preferable, but clearly I was wrong. The queen's secrets will die with her now." He held the letter over the fire.

Anna staggered forward in alarm. "No!"

"Stop!"

Hans and Anna turned around. Lord Peterssen was standing in the open door with two guards by his sides.

"Take the prince away!" Lord Peterssen demanded.

"I . . . Lord . . ." Hans looked around for an escape. "Sir, you don't understand. If you knew the truth, you'd see that this is the only way."

"I've heard everything I need to." Lord Peterssen's eyes flickered to Anna's. "And Princess Elsa tried to tell me the rest." He smiled softly. "Hello again, Anna."

Anna stepped toward him. He looked familiar too. She opened her mouth to speak and heard the window's rattling increase. She turned to look, and suddenly the window shattered. The glass flew through the room, a piece slamming into Lord Peterssen and knocking him to the ground. Hans protected his head but was hit by a piece of the window frame. The guards rushed to help the lord up as wind howled through the room, knocking portraits off the wall and sending snow everywhere. That was when Anna saw it. . . .

The letter had fallen out of Hans's hand.

Anna snatched it before it blew away and staggered out of the room, determined to find her way to the dungeons below.

CHAPTER TWENTY-EIGHT

Kristoff

Kristoff had barely ridden Sven out of the Valley of the Living Rock when he saw what was happening in the distance: the storm appeared to be directly over the castle. A swirl of white smoke rose like a cyclone before it shot out like a blast, causing a fierce wind to roar through the countryside and send birch trees sideways. Kristoff and Sven braced for impact, feeling the storm wash over them. His gut told him these new weather conditions weren't natural. They involved magic.

And curses.

Getting to Arendelle fast became even more important.

"Come on, boy!" Kristoff kicked his legs into Sven's hide.

He and Sven rode faster than they ever had before, racing into the wind down the mountainside. His hat was lost halfway down, and he could hardly see what was in front of him due to the blinding snow. The journey felt like it took forever. When Sven finally hit the bottom of the mountain, he skidded out onto what should have been the fjord. Up close, the cyclone of snow and ice looked even more menacing. It swirled toward them, and Kristoff and Sven raced right into it, bracing themselves for whatever would come.

All that mattered was reaching Anna.

Anna, with her bright smile, bubbly enthusiasm, big eyes, and need to fill every moment with chatter.

Anna, with her feisty nature and strong will that had saved him from the wolves . . . and cost him his sleigh.

Anna, who was willing to risk her life to save her village and help a princess she didn't *think* she knew.

Leave it to him to wait till now to realize he was falling for her.

And he might be too late.

"Come on, buddy! Faster!" Kristoff encouraged Sven as they sped across the fjord. He did a double take.

They were riding past what appeared to be the bow of a large ship submerged in ice. Through the driving snow, several more ships appeared like ghosts, their masts cracking in the extreme cold.

Kristoff heard the snap before he knew what was happening. By the time he looked up, a massive ship was starting to fall right toward them. It was too late to get out of the way. All Kristoff could do was lead Sven straight through, ducking as debris rained down on their heads. They cleared the ship right before it crashed, but the force still caused the ice around them to splinter. Kristoff saw the crack spreading beneath them till there was nothing but water in front of them. Sven pitched forward, sending Kristoff flying onto a sheet of ice. Sven plunged into the water.

"Sven!" Kristoff shouted, searching frantically for his best friend.

Sven broke through the icy water, clambering to pull himself up onto a nearby piece of drift ice.

Kristoff exhaled with relief. "Good boy," he shouted. "Stay there!" He struggled to stand in the fierce wind and looked around to get his bearings. Spotting the castle in the distance, Kristoff braced himself against the wind and headed toward it, hoping Anna was okay.

CHAPTER TWENTY-NINE
Elsa

"Lord Peterssen!" Elsa cried. "Kai? Gerda? Someone let me out! Please!"

No one answered.

Through the bars of the small dungeon window she noticed torches flickering in the hallway. The wind howled between the bricks, nearly blowing the flames out. Even her chains were starting to freeze, making it hard to move.

She was trapped.

Elsa sat down on the bench and stared at the metal shackles on her hands.

She couldn't just watch as her entire kingdom became a frozen tundra. She needed someone to find Anna and tell her the truth about her past. Maybe, just maybe, it would help her remember who she really was. Then the curse would break and . . . what did that mean for the weather?

Even if Anna knew who she was, Grand Pabbie had said nothing about her sister being able to stop this winter. Elsa had created it. Only she could end it.

Elsa flung her head back against the wall and heard the ice crack. Why didn't she know how to reverse the spell she had created?

I know what fear is doing to your magic, she heard Grand Pabbie say. *You must concentrate on controlling your powers.*

What did he mean by fear? She wasn't afraid of her powers, was she? What she was afraid of was not having her sister in her life. If she let Anna go, would the storm stop?

She wasn't sure, and she didn't know whom to ask.

She had lost Mama and Papa, alienated her people, and abandoned Olaf in her quest to escape her chains. There was no one left to help her.

Elsa hung her head and wept. "Mama, Papa, please help me."

The only voice she heard was the wind's.

"Princess Elsa!"

Elsa opened her eyes and stood up, straining against her chains. Someone was calling for her. It was a girl. But she didn't recognize the voice.

"Princess Elsa, where are you?"

"I'm here!" Elsa cried. It didn't sound like Gerda or Olina, but it didn't matter who it was. Someone was coming for her. "Follow my voice!"

"Found you!" The girl stuck her face in the bars and looked into the dungeon.

Elsa couldn't believe what she was seeing. The girl in front of her had red hair and blue eyes. They locked gazes, and Elsa's cuffs began to glow. Strangely, they didn't freeze up. The ice melted away. "Anna?" Elsa whispered, momentarily forgetting everything else.

"Yes." She grasped the bars. "I'm Anna. . . . Hi."

Anna wasn't a figment of her imagination. She wasn't a ghost. She was real and on the other side of the dungeon door. Elsa's younger sister was here. The curse was broken! She started to cry. "You know who I am?"

Anna paused. "Yes."

"You remember?" Elsa's tears came faster. "You remembered and you found me."

"I . . . This place . . ." Anna trailed off. She held·up a piece of parchment. "I have the queen's letter."

Elsa's cuffs glowed brighter. "You have the letter? How?" Now they could read Mama's letter together! "It doesn't matter. All that matters is you're back! You're . . . real."

"So are you," Anna whispered. They continued to

stare at each other, the only sounds coming from the storm raging outside.

Then came the sound of someone giggling.

"And so am I!"

Anna picked something up and held it in front of the bars. It was a snowman's head. The head grinned toothily.

"Olaf!" Elsa exclaimed. "You're all right!"

"Yes!" Olaf frowned. "But I left your room. I know I'm not supposed to."

"It's all right." Elsa laughed through her tears.

"And I found Anna!" Olaf said happily. "We came to find you with Kristoff and Sven, but then Kristoff and Sven left and we went off with Prince Hans."

"Hans?" Elsa's smile faded. "Where is he?" she demanded. "Anna, you can't listen to him!"

Anna opened her mouth to respond, and someone pulled her and Olaf from view.

"Anna!" Elsa cried.

"Get away from me!" she heard Anna yell.

"I can't see! I can't see!" Olaf shouted. "Put me back together!"

Elsa heard a key turn and watched the dungeon door open. Olaf's head rolled into the room without his body. Hans walked in behind it, holding Anna like his prisoner. There was a fresh cut above his right eye. "Well, isn't this refreshing?" he said. "A reunion between two sisters."

"Let her go! You can't hurt us," Elsa shouted as her cuffs glowed bright blue. "She remembers everything!"

Hans smiled. "Does she now? Let's see about that."

He pushed Anna forward. She crashed into Elsa, then fell backward, gasping for air. Ice formed on her feet and began to creep up her legs.

The curse—it wasn't broken.

Hans watched, unfazed, as the ice started to travel up Anna's body and her hair turned completely white. Anna was freezing from the inside out. Elsa strained against her chains to get away, but she couldn't go far enough.

"Anna!" Olaf panicked, his head rolling toward her.

"You'll kill her!" Elsa screamed.

Hans didn't move. "Exactly." He looked at Elsa as Anna writhed on the floor in pain. "You doomed yourself, but she was dumb enough to go after you. Now you'll both be out of the picture and I'll rule Arendelle on my own."

"*No!*" Elsa cried out in agony. Her cuffs began to glow again. Snowflakes spread across them, the chains, and soon the walls. Hans looked up in surprise as the room filled with ice. Elsa yanked once, twice, and then a third time as icicles formed on the ceiling and fell on top of them. Olaf clambered onto Anna just as the ice began to fall. Hans covered his head with his hands.

Elsa concentrated on the window in the dungeon, and willed her magic to create a hole. Finally, the stones burst, taking half the wall and her chains along with it. Each cuff on her hands broke in two, freeing her from her binds. Elsa climbed through the opening in the wall and looked back at Anna. The ice on her body was starting to recede as Elsa ran into the tempest and disappeared.

CHAPTER THIRTY

Anna

There was a loud blast and shouting, then the sound of men running.

"The princess has escaped!" someone yelled, but his voice sounded far away.

A moment earlier, Anna had felt like she was freezing from the inside out. The second Elsa was gone, the nausea subsided and she started to warm up again.

How strange, she thought.

Do the magic! the small voice inside her head said again, causing an instant headache. She tried to block the memory out.

You remember? Elsa had asked. Anna had been so surprised by the question she hadn't known how to answer her. Elsa clearly did, but Anna was still figuring out these new memories and the information Hans had fed her. She couldn't believe it was all true: she was the lost princess of Arendelle and King Agnarr and Queen Iduna's child. She thought of the portrait she had seen of the royal family in the castle.

Anna heard her heart pounding as she started to put together the pieces: the way Freya had perished, the infrequent visits under the cloak of darkness, the carriage that waited for her outside the bakery. The portrait of the queen in the castle that looked remarkably like the woman who had been her aunt and her mother's best friend.

Could Freya and the queen be the same person?

And was that person her birth mother?

She watched through the fuzz in her vision as Olaf's head rolled by and connected with his body. Suddenly it became clear: Freya *was* Queen Iduna.

The snowman poked her with his carrot nose. "Anna? Are you all right?"

Anna struggled to sit up and answer him. Then she heard someone else talking.

"Prince Hans!" A guard was leaning over a figure on the ground a few feet away.

"The princess," Hans choked out. "I tried to stop her from making the storm worse, but she struck me with her magic. She's . . . getting . . . away."

"Liar!" Anna said, but her voice was weak. The room

slowly began to come into focus. Snow was streaming into the dungeon through a large hole in the wall.

Hans pointed to Anna. "Elsa struck Anna, too. Her whole body started to freeze."

Elsa hadn't struck her. She had been happy to see Anna. But why had she run away?

Elsa, wake up! Wake up! Wake up! a voice inside her head said. *Do you want to build a snowman?*

It was her own voice from long ago. The memories were coming to the surface faster now. *I need to find Elsa.*

"Men, aid Anna while I go after the princess," she heard Hans say.

"No!" Anna shouted out as the guards descended on her. She watched as Hans turned his shoulder into the wind and disappeared through the hole. His sword was raised, ready to attack. *He's going to kill her,* Anna thought. *I have to stop him.* "I'm fine," she told the guards. "Someone needs to stop Prince Hans! He's going to hurt the princess!" The guards looked at her in confusion.

"After the princess!" one of the guards shouted and headed through the hole. The others followed.

Anna struggled to stand up, but she felt like she had been hit by something hard. Slowly, she moved toward the opening in the wall. "We have to find Elsa before Hans and the others do," Anna told Olaf, but the words sounded strange.

"Hey! Your lips are blue!" Olaf commented.

"Olaf? You have to help me get to Elsa fast. It's important!"

Olaf beamed. "Okay! I'm ready. Let's go!" He wandered off ahead of her through the wall.

Anna struggled to find her footing as she made her way through the wall and into the snow. The wind was howling. She couldn't see Olaf even though he was walking right in front of her. Around her, she could hear things creaking and falling. A sudden gust blew her backward. Olaf was lifted into the air, the three pieces of his body separating.

"Keep going!" he shouted as his parts blew away.

Anna held her arm in front of her face and turned into the wind. She needed to find Elsa before it was too late.

CHAPTER THIRTY-ONE

Elsa

Elsa spun around, unsure of her direction. Her cape blew in front of her face and she pushed it away.

The storm was so fierce there was nowhere left to shelter.

She couldn't go back to the castle. She was an enemy to her people and to Anna now.

The curse still ruled Anna's life.

Elsa's life was in ruins.

She couldn't save her people from her madness.

She didn't know how to save her sister.

She was at a loss on how to stop the storm, no matter how desperately she wanted to.

She'd never been more frightened or alone.

Elsa wandered around in the swirling darkness, barely making out the ship frozen in front of her. *Let them come for me,* she thought. *Without Anna, I've got nothing left to fight for.*

CHAPTER THIRTY-TWO

Anna

She'd lost Olaf, she couldn't see where she was going, a ship had just appeared before her like a mirage, and Elsa was nowhere to be seen. She heard a bang and watched in horror as the ship's mast tumbled into the ice and shattered, sending large chunks of ice flying. She raised her hands to her face to protect herself.

It felt like the world was ending, but she refused to let it.

There was so much to live for. She had a past to remember and a sister to get to know. Arendelle needed both its princesses. Maybe together they could bring back the sun.

Anna pulled her cape tightly around her for warmth,

but it did nothing. The cold felt like it was inside her bones, just like it had when she'd been in the room with Elsa. Something was causing this new condition, and it wasn't just the weather. Her pale hands were starting to freeze, small ice crystals forming on her wrists and fingertips.

Cursed.

Was that what was happening to her and Elsa? Had she been cursed to be kept apart from her sister? Was that why her birth parents had separated them? Maybe the queen's letter explained what had happened.

The letter!

Anna felt her dress pockets, but the letter was gone. During the explosion and Elsa's escape, it must have fallen out of her pocket. Now she had nothing that proved who she really was. Elsa was the only one who could help her, and she had run off. What if Hans found her before Anna could?

Anna slipped on the ice. There was so much of it, and slowly, she was becoming a part of it. *Please,* she begged, calling on Freya's memory—her mother's memory—to guide her. *Let me find Elsa.*

She felt an irresistible urge to turn around.

Elsa was huddled on the ground, feet from where Anna stood, with her head in her hands. Hans was standing over her. Did Elsa even know he was there? Or had she given up? *No, Elsa!* she wanted to cry out. *I . . . I remember,* she realized.

A feeling came over her, so strong that for the smallest of moments, it warmed her soul. Pictures flew through her mind: She and Elsa talking in their bedroom, baking with their mother in the kitchen, running down the central staircase. *Do the magic!* she heard a voice say, and now she realized it was her younger self begging Elsa to create more snow. Together they had skated around the Great Hall and made snow angels. They had built Olaf! She used to marvel at Elsa's magic and always wanted her sister to use it. *Do the magic!* she heard herself beg again, and then she saw the moment when everything changed. In her haste to stop Anna from falling off a snow mound, Elsa had accidentally struck her. That was when she and Elsa had been ripped apart.

She remembered everything! She—

She looked up. Hans had his sword high over his head and was about to plunge it straight into Elsa's heart.

Her sister's heart.

With what little strength she had left, Anna lunged forward.

"No!" Anna shouted, sliding in front of Elsa as the blade began to fall. She raised her hand to stop him and felt the

ice spread from her chest to her extremities. Her fingertips connected with the sword just as they froze, shattering the blade into pieces. A shock wave seemed to emanate from her frozen body, sending Hans flying backward.

Anna exhaled a last breath that evaporated into thin air.

CHAPTER THIRTY-THREE

Elsa

The vibrations rocked the ground, startling Elsa, who had been lost in her own thoughts of despair. The storm had suddenly ceased, along with the snow. Flakes were suspended in the air as if time had stopped. It took Elsa a moment to realize why.

"Anna!" she screamed, jumping up.

Her sister had turned to ice.

Anna looked like a statue, forever preserved with one hand outstretched to the sky. Her cape was frozen in motion, like she had run to Elsa's side to protect her. Hans lay a few feet away, his sword near his side. Realization struck her: Anna had stopped Hans from hurting her. She had given her life to save Elsa's.

Elsa gingerly reached out to touch Anna's frozen face. "Oh, Anna. No. No. Please, no." Her hands caressed Anna's icy cheeks.

The curse had lifted a second too late. How could magic be so cruel? *Anna. Sweet, beautiful Anna,* she thought. *It's not fair. Don't leave me.*

Elsa threw herself at Anna's frozen sculpture, crying with abandon. She didn't hear Olaf walk up beside her. She barely noticed the devastated blond man who had just arrived with a reindeer. Through the haze of the unearthly stillness, she thought she saw Lord Peterssen, a bandage around his right arm, and Gerda, Kai, and Olina on a castle balcony, watching from above. But what did any of it matter?

Perhaps the entire kingdom had just woken up from a dreamlike state and remembered: Arendelle did not have one princess. It had two. They'd found their lost princess only to lose her all over again.

I'm so sorry, Anna, Elsa thought as she clung to her sister and tears streamed down her cheeks. *I love you more than anything in this world, and I always will.* Suddenly Elsa heard a gasp and felt Anna collapse in her arms. She was alive! Her body had thawed completely. Even the white stripe in her hair had disappeared.

"Anna!" Elsa cried in surprise, looking into her sister's eyes.

Anna gripped her. "I remember *you*. I remember everything," she said, and finally they were able to embrace.

When Elsa finally pulled away, she looked at Anna with fresh eyes. "You sacrificed yourself for me," she said softly.

"I love you," Anna said, holding Elsa's hand tightly in her own. She noticed Elsa staring at something and turned around. "Kristoff!"

"Princess," he said. "There *was* a Princess Anna, and you're her. I can't believe it. I mean, I can, but . . . you're actually a princess! Am I supposed to bow? Kneel? I'm not sure what to do here."

"Don't be ridiculous! I'm still me," Anna told Kristoff with a laugh, and hugged him.

Elsa couldn't believe what she was hearing. If Kristoff knew who Anna truly was, then all of Arendelle and the kingdom did, too. Her eyes filled with tears.

"Grand Pabbie was right—love can really thaw any curse," Kristoff said.

"Love can thaw . . ." Elsa repeated. "Of course!"

All that time she had allowed herself to be wrapped up in fear—fear of being alone, fear of never finding Anna, fear of destroying the kingdom with her powers. That fear had held her prisoner since she had learned she had magic inside her. It was just as Grand Pabbie had said: she needed to learn to control her magic. If only she embraced the beauty in her life and the magic she'd been gifted—gifted, not cursed with!—then she could move mountains.

Or at least thaw out the countryside.

Elsa stared at her hands in wonder. The answer had been right in front of her all that time. "Love!"

"Elsa?" Anna questioned.

Elsa thought hard about what she was feeling; it was pure joy mixed with the greatest love she had ever known. She had a sister she loved fiercely. Focusing on that love and the love she had for her parents and her people calmed her once-frightened soul. It was her job to protect her kingdom, and she could do that now.

Her loving thoughts made her fingers tingle like they always did when she used her magic, but this time her body felt different. Her fingers began to warm.

Elsa lifted her hands to the sky, and snowflakes began to rise from the ice beneath their feet. The flakes turned into water and rose like a geyser. Everywhere she could see, all the way to the horizon, the ice was rising into the sky and evaporating. The fjord was thawing, allowing ships to be free to sail once more. Elsa hadn't even noticed that she was standing on the bow of a ship herself till it began to rise out of the ice with Anna, Kristoff, Olaf, the reindeer, and her on it.

The blue glow from her fingers continued to travel,

reaching across the water into the village. Slowly, houses that had been almost buried in snow came back to life. Flowers bloomed again, and the countryside and mountains returned to their green selves. People stepped outside in wonder as the world turned from winter to summer once more.

When the thaw was finally complete, the remaining water that had lifted into the sky swirled and spinned into a giant snowflake. Elsa gave a final wave of her hands, and the snowflake exploded in a ball of light. The sky was blue, and the sun finally showed its face again.

Anna looked at Elsa with pride. "I knew you could do it."

"Hands down, the best day of my life," Olaf agreed, his personal flurry the only remaining precipitation to be found.

Elsa heard moaning and noticed Hans clutching his jaw. She immediately started marching over. Anna reached out to stop her. "He's not worth your time," Anna said as she approached the prince herself.

Hans saw her and gasped in surprise. "Anna?" He stood up straight. "But the curse—I saw you turn to ice!"

Anna's expression hardened. "You're the one who's cold as ice!" She turned to walk away, then apparently thought better of it and punched him in the jaw.

Hans fell backward, flipping over the side of the ship and landing in the water.

They heard a cheer in the distance. Elsa looked toward the castle and saw Kai, Gerda, and several others standing on the balcony. The sight of them applauding Hans's comeuppance made her hopeful that they knew the truth about the prince. He couldn't be trusted, but she'd make sure the people of Arendelle knew they could put their faith in her once more.

"Princess Elsa!"

Elsa rushed to the side of the ship to see who was calling to her. A small boat was headed toward them, manned by two guards and Lord Peterssen. The boat bumped against the side of the ship, and Lord Peterssen climbed up while the guards stayed back to fish Hans out of the water. Lord Peterssen looked from Anna to Elsa before rushing forward to embrace them both.

His eyes were red, as if he'd been crying. "To see both princesses of Arendelle together . . . The kingdom will rejoice! People are flooding the castle—the kingdom has thawed from its deep freeze! Summer has returned thanks to you." He wiped his eyes and touched Anna's arm. "Our lost princess has been returned to us. It's as if I've lived two lives—one where I've been asleep and forgotten you and one where you're here with us again. The curse has been lifted."

"How do you know about the curse?" Elsa asked in surprise.

Lord Peterssen pulled a piece of parchment out of his jacket pocket. "I read about it in your mother's letter, which I found in the dungeons after you both ran off." He handed it to Elsa. "I wanted to make sure you got it back. Words of wisdom from the queen should not be forgotten."

"Thank you." Elsa stared at the letter she had thought she would never see again. "I never even got a chance to read it before . . ."

"You froze the kingdom?" Olaf asked, and they laughed.

"Why don't we read it together?" Anna asked, touching the parchment in wonder.

The others stepped away to give the sisters space. Elsa and Anna sat side by side on the deck and read the words their mother had written long before.

Our darling Elsa,

If you're reading this, we're gone. Otherwise, our dear girl, you would already know about the curse that separated our family long ago. We have always wanted to tell you the truth about what happened that night, but Grand Pabbie—the leader of the trolls whose wisdom we sought for help—told us the curse would someday lift and you would remember everything on your own.

As I write this, that day has not come. This is a secret we've hidden for years, and now it is hidden away here in your new lockbox, to make sure you know the truth if we are not around to give it.

You have a younger sister, Anna, who, like you, has lived in the dark far too long. We love you and your sister very much, but circumstance forced us to keep you apart. This will be hard to hear, but you were given the gift of magic that allows you to create ice and snow. When you were young, your magic accidentally struck Anna. To save her life, we sought out the wisdom of the trolls, traveling to the Valley of the Living Rock. Their leader, Grand Pabbie, was able to help Anna, but when he tried to erase her memories of your magic for her own safety, you got upset and interfered. When your magic combined with Grand Pabbie's, it cursed you and Anna differently. For you, your magic became dormant. Grand Pabbie said it would appear again when you needed your sister more than you ever had before. But for Anna, the curse meant she could not be near you, or she would turn to ice. Until the curse lifts, you and Anna must not meet.

I know you will have many questions. Too many,

I fear, for us to answer in one letter, but know you weren't separated from each other out of fear. We did what we did because we had no choice. We loved you both too much to see you hurt, and Grand Pabbie gave us a way to protect you both.

Please understand, when I say curse, I don't mean your powers. Your powers are a gift that I hope by now your father and I have helped you learn how to control.

So why tell you now? This letter serves to give you hope. You are not alone in the world! You are a smart, resourceful girl, Elsa, and I know you can find a way to reach your sister even when she is out of sight. And Anna, with her warm heart and kind soul, will find her way back to you. Other than your father and I, the family caring for Anna are the only ones who know you are sisters. The rest of Arendelle does not remember their lost princess. Grand Pabbie also hid both of your memories of each other to ease the pain of separating you. Once the magic fades, your memories will return.

If only you could have seen yourselves as children! Thick as thieves, and so inseparable that most mornings we would find Anna had crawled from her bed into yours. You were a wonderful big sister, and you will be again.

You two will find your way back to each other,
I'm sure of it. You are, and always have been, each
other's light in the darkness.
Mama and Papa

Elsa looked at Anna. They both had tears in their eyes.
They embraced again and didn't let go.

CHAPTER THIRTY-FOUR

Elsa

It took a few days for things in Arendelle to get back to normal.

Make that a new normal.

The people welcomed both of their lost princesses back with open arms.

Elsa, contrite for what had accidentally happened to the kingdom, worked tirelessly to make things right. For her first order of business, she sent Prince Hans packing.

"We shall return this scoundrel to his country," a ship captain told Elsa as they stood at the docks. "We will see what his twelve big brothers think of his behavior."

"Elsa, please let me make things right between us," Hans begged as they lead him onto the ship. He smiled apologetically. "Can't we talk?"

"Oh, I think we've done enough talking," Elsa told him. "Your brothers might hear you out, though, after they read my letter." She held a note in her hand and handed it to the captain of the ship. "I told them everything that happened here. Maybe you can convince them not to toss you into the dungeons." His face froze. "Enjoy the Southern Isles, Prince Hans."

The captain pushed Hans onto the ship. She hoped they'd never see the likes of him again.

The Duke of Weselton, however, put up more of a fight.

"This is unacceptable!" Elsa heard the Duke shouting as he was led onto a ship along with his men. "I have been a victim of fear!" the Duke argued. "I have been traumatized and—*aaah!* My neck hurts. Is there a doctor I could see?"

"You can see one when you arrive at home," Elsa told him, feeling satisfied. "Arendelle will henceforth and forever no longer do business of any sort with *Weaseltown*."

"It's Weselton!" the Duke cried as he was taken away. "Weselton!"

CHAPTER THIRTY-FIVE

Anna

While Elsa prepared for a new coronation and worked on fixing things in the kingdom, Anna took a few days to travel home to her village and see her parents. Kristoff escorted her and was surprised that the villagers were as excited to see him as they were Anna. The two of them spent a long night in front of the fire, telling everyone about their journey and about the curse that had separated the princesses. But mostly, they marveled at Tomally and Johan for so faithfully keeping the king and queen's secret. When the fire died down, people retired to their homes, and Kristoff and Sven headed to the barn. (Kristoff said he was most comfortable there.) Then Anna sat with her adoptive parents in their living room and heard the story of how she had arrived on their doorstep. Her parents weren't sure if she'd ever been kissed by a troll, but they knew trolls had played a part in her journey.

"Leaving you with me was the hardest thing your mother and father ever did, but they did it out of love," Ma told her. "We were entrusted with keeping you safe till the time came for you all to be reunited."

"She started to think that day would never come," Papa added. "I always held out hope you'd be reunited. But then . . ."

"The king and queen perished at sea," Anna finished.

Accepting what had happened to her parents would take time. Knowing she'd lost so many years with them was painful, but she reminded herself that she'd had her mother in her life without even realizing it. "Freya" had loved her fiercely, and so had Tomally and Johan. Her life had been blessed in so many ways. Finding the joy in their shared stories kept the tears at bay.

"So you mean to tell me that in all the years "Freya" visited, no one noticed she was actually the queen?" Anna asked her parents.

Ma laughed. "One time, Mr. Larson came into the shop while she was here, and he actually bowed because he was so certain she was the queen, but your father convinced him otherwise."

"I said she was a distant cousin with terrible breath," Papa told her. "That made him leave!"

The three of them roared with laughter, and Anna knew without a shadow of a doubt that they truly were her parents in every sense of the word. How fortunate she was to have had two sets of parents who loved her enough to set her free.

Anna left the village with promises to return and talk of Ma and Papa visiting her at the castle.

"We wouldn't miss your sister's coronation for the world," Ma said, hugging her tightly before letting her go to Kristoff, who was waiting to take her home. It was nice to see him out of his snow clothes, which he'd traded for a teal shirt and black vest. His blond hair shone bright in the sunlight.

Home. It felt strange to use that word about a place she hadn't lived in since she was a child, but the castle felt more familiar than she had expected. She quickly became reacquainted with the layout, her bedroom, and all the other rooms, even visiting her old friend Joan in the portrait gallery. The truth was, home was anywhere Elsa was.

She just hoped someone else would be comfortable staying nearby, too.

"Okay, here we are!" Anna said.

"*Now* can you unblindfold me?" Kristoff grumbled.

He'd spent the last half hour of their journey back to

the kingdom unable to see. Anna didn't want to ruin the surprise, so she had insisted he let her lead the way. Now they were standing on the waterfront.

"Yes!" She pulled the blindfold off. "Ta-da! I got you a new sled to replace the one that got destroyed."

Kristoff's jaw dropped. "Are you serious?"

Anna squealed excitedly. "Yes! And it's the latest model."

It wasn't just a sled. It was a state-of-the-art custom-built sleigh that had so much varnish Kristoff would never have to polish it with spit. Sven marched in front of it, almost as if the sled had been his doing. She'd wrapped the sleigh with a ribbon and placed a new lute on the seat. There was also a sack in the back of the sled filled with an ice ax, rope, and everything she could think of that he'd lost.

"I can't accept this," Kristoff said, blushing.

"You have to!" Anna insisted. "No returns! No exchanges. Future queen Elsa's orders. She's named you the official Arendelle ice master and deliverer."

She pointed to a shiny silver medal hanging from Sven's neck.

Kristoff scoffed. "That's not a thing."

"Sure it is!" Anna said. Call it a sisterly bond, but even without Anna's saying so, Elsa seemed to know how much Anna wanted Kristoff around. "And," she said, hoping to sweeten the deal, "it even has a cup holder. Do you like it?"

"Like it?" Kristoff swung Anna high in the air. "I love it! I could kiss you." He quickly put her down and ran a hand through his hair. "I mean, I could. I'd like to. May I? We me? I mean, may we? Wait. What?"

Anna leaned in and kissed Kristoff on the cheek. "We may."

Kristoff didn't hesitate. He pulled Anna into his arms and kissed her the way Anna had always imagined he would. Anna threw her arms around his neck and kissed him right back.

CHAPTER THIRTY-SIX
Anna & Elsa

After a storm comes the sun.

Arendelle truly had a new beginning, and people couldn't wait to celebrate the kingdom's rebirth. Villagers flooded the castle to celebrate not only Elsa's coronation but their lost princess. Anna had been returned to them. After so much sadness, Arendelle was basking in joy. The sisters' silhouettes appeared on new banners hanging from every flag post in the kingdom.

And when it was finally time for Elsa to stand in front of the bishop and accept her crown, Anna was exactly where she was always meant to be: right by Elsa's side.

"Queen Elsa of Arendelle!" the bishop declared as he presented her to the people in the chapel.

Elsa beamed with pride as she held the scepter and orb

in her hands. Her fingers didn't tingle and she felt no fear. She knew now her purpose was to serve her people, and she'd do it with every fiber of her being.

After the ceremony, there was a banquet in the Great Hall with a large chocolate fountain and a beautiful cake. There was dancing, laughter, and merriment. The castle itself seemed to sigh with contentment. For so long, the castle had lived in sorrow. Now it truly was a happy place.

While people enjoyed one another's company, Elsa and Anna slipped away to the entrance hall and studied their family's newly restored royal portrait. The one with the king, the queen, Elsa, and Anna had been returned to its rightful place of honor. Mr. Ludenburg had already declared that he would complete a new sculpture for the castle courtyard fountain that reflected the family of four.

"Tell me something about them I don't know," Anna said as she slipped her arm through Elsa's.

Anna asked her questions like that daily, and Elsa loved to answer them. The two stayed up late into the night, sitting on each other's beds, talking about anything and everything they could imagine.

"They loved sweets almost as much as you and I do," Elsa said as they turned to walk back toward the party. "Especially krumkaker."

Anna grinned. "I remember baking those! You always

ate half the batter before Miss Olina could cook them."

"That was you!" Elsa said accusingly, laughing.

"Maybe it was Mama," Anna said, but she was laughing, too.

Kristoff and Olaf watched the sisters from the doorway with smiles.

No one seemed to want the party to end, so it didn't. Not for a long while. But when the banquet hall grew warm and people needed air, Elsa knew exactly what to do to help them cool off. She gathered everyone outside.

"Are you ready?" Elsa asked the crowd.

Their cheers and applause told her all she needed to know.

Her magic no longer felt like a shackle. It was truly a gift, as her mother had always told her, and now she used it with joy instead of fear.

Elsa tapped her foot on the courtyard ground. A sheet of ice slowly spread throughout the plaza. Next Elsa lifted her hands to the sky and made the lightest of snowflakes fall. On a hot summer night like that, an impromptu ice-skating party was the perfect gift.

People skidded around the square, enjoying the magic she had long kept to herself. Anna slid into place beside her.

"This is so much fun!" Anna smiled. "I'm so happy I'm here with you."

Elsa held her arm tight. "We will never be apart again," she promised. Then she transformed Anna's shoes into an elegant pair of ice skates.

"Oh, Elsa, they're beautiful, but you know I don't skate," Anna said.

Elsa grabbed her arms and swung her around the ice. "Come on!" she said, shouting encouragement to her little sister. "You can do it!" The two of them laughed as they spun around the fountain in the courtyard.

"I got it! I got it! I don't got it!" Anna laughed as she kept slipping.

"Look out! Reindeer coming through!" said Kristoff as he and Sven slid by.

"Hey, guys!" Olaf joined them on the ice. "Glide and pivot! Glide and pivot!" he advised as he grabbed hold of Elsa's cape and went for a spin around the square.

Elsa smiled, her heart full and her head in a good place. Her people were happy. She was content. And she was very, very loved by a sister who had finally been returned to her. Things were exactly as they should be.

Twisted Tales

Unravel new twists in the tales that you already know and love in this series of thrilling novels.

Reflection

What if Mulan had to travel to the Underworld?

Still disguised as the soldier Ping, Mulan faces
a deadly battle in a mysterious world as she
tries to save the life of Captain Shang.

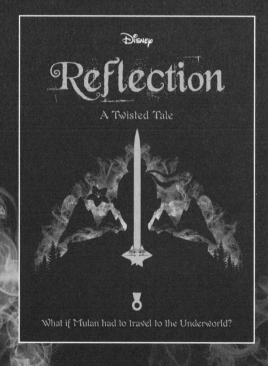

Part of Your World

What if Ariel had never defeated Ursula?

With evil Ursula ruling Prince Eric's kingdom on
land, it's up to Ariel – now the voiceless queen of
Atlantica – to overthrow the murderous villain.

Mirror, Mirro

What if the Evil Queen poisoned the p

Can Snow defeat an enemy who will st
at nothing to retain her power… includ
going after the ones Snow loves?

Disney

Mirror, Mirror

A Twisted Tale

What if the Evil Queen poisoned the prince?